THE SHANGHAI GESTURE

a novel by
GARY INDIANA

TWO DOLLAR RADIO
Since *2005

The Shanghai Gesture
A Novel by Gary Indiana
Copyright 2009 by Gary Indiana
ISBN: 978-0-9820151-0-0
LCCN: 2009900937

Cover by Barbara Kruger.
Layout by Two Dollar Radio.

Distributed to the trade by
Consortium Book Sales & Distribution, Inc.
34 Thirteenth Avenue NE, Suite 101
Minneapolis, Minnesota 55413-1007
www.cbsd.com
phone 612.746.2600 | fax 612.746.2606
orders 800.283.3572

TWO DOLLAR RADIO
Since *2005
www.TwoDollarRadio.com
twodollar@TwoDollarRadio.com

For Susan De Palma

"It took more than one man to change my name to Shanghai Lily."

Marlene Dietrich, *Shanghai Express*

THE SHANGHAI GESTURE

PART ONE

Ningpo More Far

Among Those That Know, a cabal our story will elucidate in the fullness of time, rumors fluttered that Dr. Obregon Petrie defied the laws of gravity when it suited his caprice.

Reports of Petrie in languorous flight through the velvet-shrouded parlors of his monstrous Victorian folly, of static levitation, even tales of Petrie clinging spiderlike to the plaster grape-and-putti moldings that lined the ornate ceilings of those musty rooms, suffocated by curio cabinets and incunabula, were rife not only in the hushed confabulations of Those That Know, but a topic of idle gossip among the raucous sailors, coney-catchers, fishwives, and floozies who trolled Gin Lane and its tributary alleys at Land's End. These were the human tidewash of any seafaring backwater, for whom no superstition is too far-fetched, and no inebriated fantasy fails to inspire lurid embellishment.

Petrie, airborne or otherwise, enjoyed much esteem at Land's End, for the storm-ravaged shipping town's human debris experienced no end of bleeding piles, recurrent malaria, scurvy, dropsy, high blood pressure, and a lowering effulgence of hardy pox, to say nothing of the port's relentless pestilence of insomnia, a veritable miasmic funk endemic to the area since the wreckage, a century earlier, of *The Ardent Somdomite*.

Obregon Petrie possessed a maestro's touch with most of

the district's repugnant, ever-recrudescent maladies, though his tinctures, creams, crystal amulets, cowpat exfoliants, vegetable poultices, infusions of sheep's urine, and like remedies provided little amelioration of the "waking dream" Land's End drifted through each day until nightfall.

Only one of Dr. Petrie's medicaments was known to relieve the diurnal somnolence and nocturnal abandon of his clientele. Alas, this balm came scarce and dear to the family exchequer, and was required for personal use by Dr. Petrie in such prodigious quantities that seldom could a drop be spared, even for those whose means might otherwise afford its purchase.

Since that long ago, mysterious collision of the *Ardent* with the archipelago of saber-toothed guano outcroppings beyond Zabriskie Harbor, the wags of neighboring Loch Stochenbaryl, East Clamcove, and Swill-upon-Mersey (communities themselves notorious for the maniacal swiving of bovine herds and poachery of game hens) cast withering execration upon our seaside enclave as "haunted."

Land's End's denizens indeed excited alarm with their sleep-starved, hallucinatory revels at eventide. Yet aside from its reversal of the customary ordering of time, Land's End was no better and no worse than other grubby, licentious coastal hamlets dependent for revenue upon hard-drinking, brawlsome, lecherous dockworkers and sailors crowding their domains.

By day, Land's End presented the chance traveller a dusty, unpeopled village, its serpentine lanes and ill-cobbled thoroughfares traversed by pariah dogs and an occasional disoriented porcupine or muskrat. At best, such a wayfarer might glimpse Dimitrios, the baker, who roused himself at cock's crow to knead and yeast the town's famous savory biscuits; Humbolt, the butcher, might be visible through a scrim of turdlike, mauve and scarlet sausages pendant in his grimy window, slamming a razor-honed cleaver into pork loins and accordionlike sides of beef; at Myshkin's Confectioners, a jewel box of delectable, fruit-pimpled cakes and fragrant pies piped their siren aroma long hours before the wild, thistled hills behind Loch Stochenbaryl engorged the dissolute afterglow of dusk.

But the veins of these night-sleeping merchants ran with foreign blood. Their ways were not the town's ways. They had suppurated from distant, oily realms, where barbarism waved its crude, intemperate sceptre. Immune to indigenous distress, their ruddy health seemed itself symptomatic of more furtive, hence more virulent inner riots of depravity.

Dimitrios was Greek, his ready smile unquestionably a pederastic leer; Humbolt, East Prussian to the core, disported all the gruff, militaristic vulgarity of his ilk; Myshkin, with his mincing feminate flourishes and constant stroking of his apron's forepart, belonged to some obscurantist Christian sect, or worse. His shanty, perched amid the phosphorescent lichen beds of Mica Slide, featured weeping icons and statuettes of apocryphal-sounding saints and starets, whom the few who'd ever ventured there presumed to be satanic fetishes and hoodoo simulacra of the townsfolk.

The ululating tongues of Gin Lane asserted that Myshkin's piety dissembled a cunning, avaricious Jew behind the confectioner's sugar with which he was usually festooned, that the dough of his cakes and eclairs was kneaded with the blood of Christian infants, and that his annual vacations were furtive trips to the Bilderberg Meetings, whose members rule the world *sub rosa*.

Such, at least, were the primitive, nugatory blatherings among the ignorant townsfolk. A few of us who lived at Land's End – not Those That Know, whose impenetrable secrecy concealed their very identities, but those of us, I mean to say, who knew Petrie – were acquainted with another side of the distinguished doctor, for Petrie's familiars regularly gathered in his rooms for evenings of bezique and the requisite blinis and caviar, washed down with flutes of French champagne, to which Petrie treated us when, almost every week, as he put it, his "ship came in ahead of schedule." What ship that was, the townspeople knew not; the Chinese coolies at the docks, however, who whiled their sparse hours' reprieve from herniating labor and the cruel lash of the harbormaster's bullwhip in Gin Lane's crapulous warrens of aromatic lassitude, knew Petrie's vessel well. But these prematurely wizened, cryptic Orientals kept their buccal orifices zipped for all but the insertion of the succoring pipe.

The motley of Petrie's acquaintances included Khartovski, a former Marxist-Leninist pamphlet-monger with a doctorate degree from the London School of Economics, which had done nothing to relieve his chronic penury. Khartovski's elongated, boneless form, its head resembling a speckled egg sprouting two taut braids of chin-length moustache, habitually draped itself athwart Petrie's green and beige striped sofa.

Sporadically, as if recalling in his cups the sylvan highlands and dales of an imaginary youth (Khartovski hailed, if that is the term, from a nameless Crimean obscurity), he declaimed Odes and Lays of the Robert Burns and Ettrick Shepherd variety in a guttural Russian accent.

Marco Dominguez, a Cameroonais of anthracite coloration, forever in demand for impromtu, unpaid repair work by Land's End's ennui-stricken grass widows, invariably joined us for bezique and regaled us with tales of bygone wildlife encounters and trophy maidenheads acquired in the bush. This nobly-hewn African émigré had amassed a fortune in small arms deals at the precocious age of twenty-two.

It was said that Marco could assemble a Kalashnikov from scattered parts in the time it takes a teakettle to raise a simmer. He dressed with a dash and flair rarely attempted in the rough-and-tumble sinkhole of our seaside purgatory, for lack of a kinder term. Marco, whose bearing suggested that of a tribal prince, wished to live the retiring life of an English gentleman from the Edwardian era, despite his much-sought, reputedly enormous dexterity and insatiable appetite for minor household repairs.

Another of Petrie's callers, Dr. Philidor Wellbutrin, was a rotund, excessively flatulent, puff-eyed OB/GYN (such, at least, was the euphemism active among the town's tarts and ostensibly virginal, unmarried daughters), whose ungovernable mane of flame red hair matched a ready tongue as fiery as his whorling tresses.

Petrie's salon further included Colecrupper, the local auto mechanic, an autodidact of vast pretentions and meager learning. These evening hands of bezique were further enlivened by visits from Thalidomido, a bow-legged, Umbrian dwarf, whose head followed the contour of a Bartlett pear, his torso that of a Bose stereo speaker. The soul of gaiety at Petrie's – save during cyclical spells of depressive rage that came upon him without warning – Thalidomido administered the local doll hospital, and reportedly terrorized its abject staff of "little people" with asperities and cutting personal remarks, alternating with melancholic, tearful vows to hurl himself from Strumpet Margot's Cliff, a crumbling extrusion of laterite on the edge of the lower town. Strumpet Margot had been driven to her end by a cavalry officer of wretched morals; the edge of the abyssal drop that bore her name was a favored setting for moonlight picnics and for carnal liaisons in motor vehicles whose owners Colecrupper derived tart, sanctimonious glee from identifying by their license plate numbers.

I do not suggest that I was Petrie's sole confidante, though because I rented a suite of rooms on his topmost floor, I "knew him" better than others. I did, in truth, pass greater time in Petrie's company than they, being young and, some said, comely as a rogue yet shy as a peacock hen, as I am afflicted with a speech disorder of a mortifying nature, and, as Petrie often teased, with a sigh of envy, "footloose and full of dreamy fancies." I was, in consequence, "more privy" (a locution I found particularly unfortunate, though the doctor intended a single entendre) to an occluded side of his existence.

With regard to many, though hardly all matters, the category of "confidante" would have encompassed much of Land's End and its periphery. Petrie could keep practically nothing to himself, even when discretion strongly recommended otherwise.

We card partners were hardly unaware that Petrie's "miracle remedy" for the town's primary ailment was clove-flavored tincture of laudanum, upon which Petrie himself had a punishingly copious dependence.

The realm of murk I alluded to just now, which Petrie kept truly secret, comprises much of my story here. He kept this realm sealed off from his other intimates and everyone for the excellent reason that his life depended on it – certain episodes of which, based entirely on the doctor's *ipsissima verba*, I record here, perhaps to no great purpose.

At the time I speak of, there lived at Land's End an orotund, balding, malicious fool of a gossiping tavern-keeper named Sauerbrotten, who rented out bungalows to nautical transients. During those rare months when our generally nauseating climate permitted, Sauerbrotten, with the portentous air of an Asiatic Potentate flaunting the takings from a pasha's ransom, threw open the fetid, weedy rear lot of his property, as what it pleased him to extoll as an "enchanting Viennese beer and wine garden" – in truth, a sorrily improvised refuse-clearing effort, embellished with wobbling third-hand tearoom furniture and Cinzano table awnings, citronella candles weakly flickering in amber globes encased in plastic mesh, offering "cocktails" in jelly glasses, colored plastic monkeys affixed to their rims by spiral tails, smouldering mosquito coils extruding where rice paper parasols or toothpick-impaled Gibson onions might have graced less squalidly flourished offerings.

The menu of this rebarbative Bavarian's groaning board featured the cuisine of his native slough, overgenerously replete with sausage meats, corpulent, tasteless grey dumplings in puddles of yellow broth, kidney dishes of indeterminable origin, fillets of boar snout, and a veritable Escoffier of spit-roasted hog products.

A waste area the remainder of the year, Sauerbrotten's

enchanted garden featured a slowly collapsing, termite-ridden, ornamented bandstand, its carved peak slumping in on itself like the crown of a marshmallow wedding cake under heavy barometric pressure, which served as an octagonal stage for shabby entertainers the malignant German enticed seawards to distract his restive, carnivorous patrons: klezmer quartets, clumsy magicians performing listless feats of prestidigitation, jongleurs, and boorish practitioners of "stand-up comedy" – most of whom were incapable of standing up by the time the entertainment hour gonged.

Of Sauerbrotten's mousy, charmless spouse, who operated this gong, I will later provide a surprising report. But that anon.

It happened that Petrie's associate and boon companion, Inspector Weymouth Nargil Smith, periodically arrived up from London on the Newcastle train or by private motorcar, sometimes passing a few days at Sauerbrotten's inn, though just as often, Smith made directly for Petrie's house and departed the same evening with Petrie in tow: often reluctantly, for Petrie fretted about his ever-growing "habituation," but Smith assuaged such fears with an ingenious combination of appeals to Petrie's altruism on behalf of humanity and an often improvised supply of "maintenance substances."

Therefore it was not unusual for Petrie to vanish from Land's End in Smith's company for many weeks, sometimes months. And dark weeks and months these were for Petrie's clientele, which fanned out all over the harbor and nearby port towns in desperate quest for chemical relief.

Petrie and Smith's connection did not go unremarked by the serpent's tooth that passed for Sauerbrotten's tongue: the implacable tub of lard would ambulate among his so-called dining tables, whose torpid occupants, engorged with fatty meats, could not have been less interested, depositing cryptic innuendos of diabolical contrivance, his favorite being a suggestion that the laconic, dignified Smith "had his clutches into Petrie, like an owl with its talons in a mouse." No stranger to the heady beverages he urged upon his customers with the rapacity of a born enabler, Sauerbrotten sometimes added hints about "unnatural ties of affection" that shepherds by a grosser name do call, practices "well known among the ancient Romans to cause earthquakes," and the like.

Weymouth Smith, whose senses were preternaturally alert to more critical matters, and who was, besides, a gentleman – that is to say, an individual of such vast independent means that he believed everyone he encountered liked him for his charm and *savoir faire* – failed ever to sense the petty animosity aroused in Sauerbrotten during his infrequent use of the innkeeper's premises.

Petrie – who hoisted the occasional pint with his mates at the Scroop of Masham, as Sauerbrotten's establishment was dubbed – himself had but the vaguest intimation of its proprietor's busy mouth, *vis-à-vis* himself and Smith. That Sauerbrotten incarnated the worst of his porcine native region, of course, was evident to anyone who set foot inside the Scroop of Masham – which, as the locals all knew, he had acquired in dowry from Erna, his mineral-like spouse, whose maiden name, Cuntze, had formerly embellished the pediment above the entrance in ormolu san serif since time immemorial; "The Whistling Cuntze" appears *en passant* in the journals of Tobias Smollett and Daniel Defoe, and Boswell records a raucous evening of disputation at "the ever-welcoming Cuntze" involving Dr. Johnson and a well-tippled local theologian. Sauerbrotten's peremptory rechristening of the legendary Cuntze in honor of Henry V's betrayer gained him no glory at Land's End, though Scottish wags derived some tepid glee from this nominal desecration.

These matters would be of naught significance, had that evanescent summer not included Sauerbrotten's hiring, as entertainment, an itinerant orchestra of young women, under the tyrannical direction of a vile, nerve-wracked, moustached impresario named Zryd.

Zryd was a horse's ass from Trieste, avarice and anemic lust doodled all over his goatish visage. This visage had seen less dissipated days in a faraway past, but the ravages of years had never registered in Zryd's frequent preenings in the mirror of his bungalow. He imagined himself, I believe, "debonair," the cynosure of all female eyes. I believe, too, that the female eyes he wished to be the cynosure of belonged to that species of bloated, blue-haired, lucratively widowed females seldom known to frequent the Scroop of Masham, though once upon a time large claques and bevies of these diamond-draped, botoxed, and well-heeled senior misses had whiled away soporific evenings at the former Whistling Cuntze.

In those days, one could engage in a hand of whist, a rubber of bridge, or promenade on the veranda without getting splashed by some sailor's projectile vomit. Dreary as she was, Erna Cuntze had come from Quality. The Sauerbrotten creature had not. And Erna was the last of the Cuntzes; their like would nevermore be seen in Northern Europe.

Zryd had himself performed on cello at the Whistling Cuntze in his youth; during the Cuntze's vulgarization into the Scroop of Masham, he had been years touring his charges throughout Micronesia. He had not, in fact, set foot on British soil in two decades. But now much of Micronesia had vanished beneath the *aqua alta*, and few of the remaining islands had need of touring entertainment.

The young ladies of the visiting orchestra, but for one exception, were neither young, nor, as far as anyone could tell, ladies, and their exertions on tubas, clarinets, piano, cello, and violin elicited from the Scroop of Masham's abundant oafs solicitations of the coarsest nature, particularly to those unluckily employed on wind instruments. Zryd inveighed his indentured mistresses of melody to "circulate" among the clientele between long bouts of cacophony – adding, as Petrie quickly noticed, to the despondency of the company's flautist, a mop-haired, incongruously attractive, raccoon-eyed young woman, whose silently challenging presence in that infernal grouping could only be accounted for by resentedly reduced circumstances.

The flautist had expressed, in whispered colloquy to certain of her colleagues in the orchestra, her sense that there was something "not right" about this place Zryd had brought them to. Indeed, she had uttered this trepidation one evening when chance landed her at a table occupied by our cohort Khartovski: as he confided to me, the normally silent girl had quietly but urgently begged him and his drinking partner that evening, the unflappable Marco, to "get her out of there" before something hideous occurred.

Petrie brought the evident plight of this intringuing ingenue to Smith's attention when the duo stopped for a sherry at the Scroop of Masham to fortify themselves for one of their motoring trips to London, unwittingly providing Sauerbrotten with no end of fresh, luridly speculative gossip. Smith noted the dismal gestalt at a glance: Zryd's exasperation at the girl's sullen demeanor, Sauerbrotten's ill-dissembled, tumescent interest in the fierce-eyed creature, and the girl's utter unlikelihood in that base, imprisoning menagerie.

Yet Smith had no time to decipher the girl's evident disgust at her situation. An urgent mission loomed, and, after knocking back their sherries, he and Petrie were bound for London.

Herewith, for a time, I shall leave the narration in Petrie's able mouth.

"This time it's urgent," Smith assured me. "Unless we make haste, and I mean haste, our boon companion in the struggle, Sir Lionel Parker, may well buy the farm before midnight!"

"Good grief, Smith, you've already told me that! Aren't we on the wrong motorway?"

"Perhaps, perhaps not. It all depends."

I considered once again the invaluable role of Sir Lionel Parker in Weymouth Smith's and, I suppose, my own comparatively adjunct one in defense of the Nation.

Sir Lionel Parker was one of the greatest Egyptologists and crossword puzzle mavens of our day. It was Sir Lionel who had deciphered the so-called Linear C, the hieroglyphic remnants of the Hyksos – those mysterious invaders who conquered the Egyptian empire on horseback, reigned for a century, and promptly disappeared. Until that time, no one had ever gleaned a clue as to where the Hyksos had come from, nor to whence they disappeared. Parker had made it his life's work to solve this archaeological riddle, thus far with mixed results.

Moreover, Sir Lionel and Weymouth Smith went "way back" – indeed, the archaeologist had mentored Smith at Scotland Yard and taught him to de-encrypt certain ciphers of an almost timeless nature; had rescued Smith from the clutches of the

Nation's foes in Egypt and Syria; moreover, Sir Lionel had taught me how to grow poppies in unfavorable climates with the use of various herbs.

"No doubt you will think me mad," said Smith, as his battered Mini Cooper roared Londonward down the motorway.

"You certainly drive like a maniac," I observed, listlessly mindful of the speedometer's climbing red needle, and Smith's ability to glaze over on a single alcoholic drink. "I think you're one over the eight, my friend. Maybe I should drive."

"Ha ha ha, Petrie, you old devil," Smith japed. "Unless I am much mistaken, you yourself are on the nod. Imagine putting you behind the wheel of a powerful motor vehicle in your condition."

Smith, as usual, pounded the nail of imperious repartee firmly into my head. As a precaution against the nerve-wracking agitation Smith's whirlwind manifestations at Land's End churned in my guts, I'd injected twice my usual dose of travel morphine before leaving the house. Now the sherry I'd imbibed was reaping havoc with my stomach. You can't win.

"I thought you were in Myanmar."

"I was, Petrie. And a ripe sewer it is, I can tell you. Worse than Burma. The noise. And the *people*." Smith shuddered. "And what I encountered there is precisely why I am now here." A long calculating silence. "Have I piqued your curiosity?"

"I have no curiosity. That's why I've elected to live in the country."

Smith chuckled unpleasantly.

"And in such a stench-ridden cloaca as Land's End, too. Notorious in its day," Smith mused, blithely passing seven cars crammed with obese vacationing families. What sordid dramas must be transpiring in those vehicles, I thought. If each passenger is twice his or her proper body weight, and the gasoline required to… what do fat people do with each other? My thoughts scattered like lawn debris in the airflow of a leafblower. Smith sheared back into the right lane, seconds short of rear-ending a lorry stuffed with potato sacks.

"The British never tire of potatoes, do they," Smith noted sourly.

"The wreck of *The Ardent Somdomite* hasn't been forgotten in the town," I said for no particular reason.

"Nor an earlier time, either." Smith's cryptic remark was wasted on me. I ignored the bait. The recessed lights in the dashboard emitted quasar-like signals from another realm. A realm of friendly, underwater silences and threadlike streaks of celestial illumination.

"One remarkable thing about you," Smith expatiated after a brief interlude of broken mufflers and horn honks, "is how a fellow of such copious erudition gleans so little of what goes on beneath his very nostrils."

I was too wrecked to take umbrage. Umbrage cut no ice with Smith, in any case, and I had no idea what he was talking about. Northbound headlights across the ice plant meridian dazzled me with interplanetary twinkling.

Yes, I thought, there is another world inside this one. If only everyone surrendered to its radiance. But that would send the price of dope through the astral plane.

"You sell your maisonette in Cheney Walk at a loss, abandon your family, then sight unseen, purchase a decrepit Victorian eyesore in the veritable anus of Great Britain's fading shipbuilding industry. Then you swallow whole this convenient twaddle about the *Somdomite* spreading narcolepsy through the countryside."

"There's really nothing convenient about narcolepsy," I yawned.

"That's where you're mistaken," Smith leered sardonically. "Epidemic, though? And you a medical doctor."

He flicked a gold lighter and drew on a cigar-leaf spliff.

"Has it never occurred to you that something more sinister

than *narcolepsy* might account for the… odd condition of this shitburg you've settled in? Think dialectically, old man, apply your empirical training. I mean, you were a licensed physician, Petrie."

"Board certified," I mumbled bitterly.

"And, had you restrained your habit of promiscuous penmanship, you'd still be on the Registry."

Landscape, black and brooding, smeared the windows like liquid tar.

"At the very least, you must know that narcolepsy isn't contagious. True, it afflicts one in nine individuals to varying degrees. But an entire *hamlet*?"

Through my morphic haze, Smith managed to get on my nerves.

"But then," he continued relentless, "you never could tell a skagged-out slag from a joint-swollen high-kicker."

Enough, I thought, is never enough for this one.

"For the thousandth time, Smith, I concede that chippie Dixie Pommeroy bamboozled yours truly with her tale of bursitic agony. I honestly did believe she was in the chorus line at the Lyric – third girl from the left, I believe she told me – afflicted with osteopathic torment. She was damned convincing. And quite a stunner, I might add. One hates to see a gal in the bloom of youth in crippling pain."

"Or such a blooming fraud busted for solicitation ten minutes after her consult, with your prescription paper-clipped to her douche bag. I'm afraid the bloom was off that rose since Biba's Kensington closed. Not to rake over old coals, my friend, but the whole shebang was a set-up, including Dixie's bust. She was trawling the sidewalk ten minutes after they took her prints. They even let her fill your script at Boots. Her little habit was no skin off their hindquarters."

"Whose hindquarters do you mean by they, who are these them, do you mean to say – "

"I mean as I speak, a set-up. Get that finally through your foggy noggin, Petrie. A scheme to get to me, by getting to you. Engineered by you know who."

The scumble of light and shadow on Smith's face resembled a speeded-up Béla Tarr movie. I could not recall who *you know who* might be, if indeed I had ever known, and, honestly, didn't give a rat's ass. I had an insatiable craving for walnut pecan ice cream, and possibly another shot.

"Now you make no sense at all, Smith. Dixie Pommeroy," I wheezed, with less than total conviction, hoping to penetrate Smith's frothy discourse with a verbal hatpin, "was a victim of circumstance. Granted, my practice was smack in the center of a pigpen of vice squad surveillance. She was also a whore, I'll grant you that, but whoredom isn't a vast stretch from the Lyric chorus line. You're an awful snob when you want to be, Smith."

Smith popped a stick of raspberry Bubblicious gum between his glistening teeth, still sucking on the plump joint.

"Then, their little scheme backfired. The idea was to lure me back to Britain to pull strings with the High Commissioner on your behalf."

"How clever of you not to do so," I said with all the acerbity I could muster. "I'd still have the inconvenience of a legitimate medical license."

"Far from it. You and I, Petrie, would both be as expired as a yellowfin in a sushi bar."

"I still don't see where Dixie Pommeroy figures into it. She was only a chorus girl."

"You mean a whore."

"All right, whore, strumpet, sleaze bag, prostitute, hooker, woman of the night, courtesan, streetwalker, ho, be-ach, track runner, call girl – I mean really, Smith. You're too much."

Smith paused for effect, ineffectually.

"That same Dixie Pommeroy you describe as just a whore,"

he whistled out, chewing gun and holding in smoke at the same time, "is operating out of Shanghai at this very moment. Making an occasional foray into Myanmar with pound bags of Chiang Mai Dreamy Dust for you know who."

I missed Dixie, suddenly. Not that I'd known her for more than twenty minutes. But she'd left a certain *je ne sais quoi* wafting through my examining room, like the scent of *Jamais de la Vie*. She'd expelled a lot of spunk, even for a girl of the streets.

Why bring the happy shit into Myanmar, I idly wondered. They have plenty of domestic product right there. Whereas at Land's End, supply often was touch and go.

The radiant nimbus of London heaved into view: its soaring monolith towers, its sprawling rebus of electronic graphics, its stroboscopic advertising zeppelins, its torn bonnet of ink blue sky smeared with brushstroke clouds, constellations, and satellites wheeling in the upper ether.

The perpetual drizzle of acid rain stained the macadam. London's ineffable stench, a potpourri of rotten fruit, ozone, car exhaust, patchouli oil, human excrement, methane, and dead fish tossed up by the jelling cesspool of the Thames, summoned images of the life I had abandoned.

"Fiona was a rancid slag," said Smith, reading my thoughts. "And I'd hardly describe that litter she dropped as human children."

I searched my scrambled mind for a comeback.

"You've never been a father," I declared. Not that I missed the little shits. Their drool, their snot-dripping snouts, their imbecile chatter, their stinking nappies. Had they even been mine?

"Oh yes I bloody have," chortled Smith. "On countless occasions."

At times, Smith's swank condescension prodded me beyond endurance.

"Slopping baby batter in every slit from here to Samarkand isn't the same as being an actual father."

Smith, unfazed, goosed the accelerator with his snakeskin espadrilles.

"I only pray we're not too late." He sucked in ganja smoke.

"Too late for what?"

"Oh, silly me. My mind is so occupied with chill apprehensions that I haven't filled you in, fleshed out the narrative. Spilled the beans. Laid the down-low dope on you."

"Planning to babble like a parrot all night, or could you kindly spit it out? Suspense is the last thing I need."

It's a rotten life, I considered, but somebody has to live it.

"If a clean syringe happens to be the first thing you need, Petrie, there's a fully loaded one in the glove box."

One thing I can say for Smith, he knew what I wanted. We entered the ever-reconfigured precincts of Limehouse. Half sewertown, half real estate Nirvana. The streets ablaze with neon and LED signage, microchip photograms coating the walls of hundreds of buildings of every vintage and elevation. The sidewalks a sculpture garden of junkies and Ninja gangs, Mohawks bristling in rainbow tints, the antique flotsam of *Blade Runner* conjoined with the boxy drab of K-Mart.

We ran an obstacle course of human wreckage, stylish plummy couples floating in and out of smart boutiques and electronics stores, luxury food marts, fashionable bistros. Some wheeled their replicants in prams, others reported their progress through space into mobiles, in screaming voices, to people they would be encountering within seconds.

"I'm right near you right now."

"I can see your ass but not your face."

Solitary males used their phones to shave. Some transmitted their clearance cards to airport check-in counters. Still others, ears grafted to iMe's, collided with utility poles and shop windows, enraptured by the iMe's menu of simultaneous functions, notorious for scrambling the user's belfry into euphoric obliviousness.

"Watch out for information loop," Smith gravely cautioned. "It's from a whole new arsenal of espionage implementa. We're either being tracked, or will be soon enough. It's a spell since you visited Shadowland, ain't it? Plenty of new toys our enemies like to fiddle with."

"I won't ask which enemies, since they seem to be legion."

"We do have plenty. Me, you, the Nation, the very vestiges of our civilization."

"What *is* information loop?"

Smith warmed to the subject as he sideswiped a parked BMW.

"An ingenious neurological tweak in the brainwash department. If you notice the same thing happening twice, like a film loop, chances are you've been zapped with a loop needle. They evaporate on contact. In which case, take one of these."

Smith handed me a small tin of lozenges.

"Loop assault makes identity theft look like pickpocketing. No forms to fill out, no numbers to punch in. You just do a *walk-in* on somebody else's brain without ever leaving your body. But it takes at least two minutes for the toxins to complete a memory wipe. Temporary erasure, but it doesn't take long to do *mucho* damage. Swallow one of these, and the process reverses itself. Or so I am told. You know I can never quite get the hang of these technical things. But perhaps, Petrie, you, with your superior medical knowledge…" Smith's voice trailed away.

I pried the lid from the tin and stared at numerous tiny, colored bubbles.

"What are they?"

"Neuron blockers. Same as beta blockers. But for synapse protection."

"What happens if you don't take one in time?"

Smith chewed his lip, sucked on his spliff, and spat his gum out the driver side window: ambidextrous with his mouth.

"Not sure how to put it. Get a Phantom Captain situation.

Almost anybody can telepath into it."

"But I mean to say, what happens to *you*?"

Smith restrained himself from raucous mirth.

"There isn't any *you*, Petrie. There isn't any *I*, either. Not in this day and age, if ever there were. Never much to all that anyway. Once you've been looped, the 'you' you think is you starts cancelling itself like a postage stamp."

He darted into a parking space near the gaudy portals of a Chinese restaurant. Amber Lotus Heavenly Eating Compartment. Standard neon signage, sinuous blinking dragon. Generic dump, more or less.

Killed the ignition. Tapped his fleshy lips. Pulled up his shirtcuff and thrust his wrist into my sightline.

By this time, my eyes barely registered single objects. The entire city seemed collapsing, like an avalanche of Christmas bulbs and edifices melting into oozing blobs.

After a few powerful slaps in the face from Smith, I focused on a nasty gash on his forearm. The flesh puffed and scarlet around the sutured cicatrice.

"Ever seen anything like this?"

I am a doctor, of course, and have seen everything.

"It's a deep puncture of some sort that's been cauterized. It also resembles a sewn-up vagina, or a rectum sealed with candle wax. Since it's on your arm, I'll go with my first guess."

"It may interest you to know, Petrie, that a stinger packed with hamadryad venom caused this gash!"

"My word, Smith! A hamadryad! The deadliest reptile or insect in the Orient!" I had never actually heard of any hamadryad inhabiting any region of Asia. The hamadryad is indigenous to South America.

"Oh," Smith sighed, "I don't know. They say the saliva of a Komodo dragon contains enough bacteria to kill you if it sneezes near you. But the Komodo is amphibious, I seem to recall. All the same, the hamadryad's poison is no day at the beach. I spent a week raving in a whorehouse that reeked of malaria, flat on my back. And I'd be there now, lifeless in Rangoon, if I hadn't acted instantly."

The mary jane fumes roiled my vision. I hallucinated a sort of soap bar of cholesterol. I remembered Smith.

"Putrid luck, to pick the one whorehouse in South Asia with a hamadryad scuttling around."

"Exactly my point, Petrie. That reptile was *planted* in that whorehouse, in the very bed I had just shared an hour earlier, unwittingly, with a will-less emissary of you know who."

Smith examined his wound thoughtfully.

"She had the most… *versatile* pleasure hole I'd plummeted in years – which ought to have aroused my suspicions. But I allowed my tumescent prong to lead me by the nose."

My crotch began itching in a tormenting manner. Smith's story sullied my high. The cold burn crept all over me, complete with pinches of imaginary bug bites.

Smith sucked his dwindling boo, holding in its fragrant effluvia, as if pushing himself to new peaks of hypervigilance.

His gaze had frozen on the restaurant window. It featured an immense aquarium where semi-comatose carp and some stunted lobsters swished and straggled through greenish water, soon to be plucked from their befouled native medium, hacked to pieces for the dining enjoyment of what appeared a table of Hong Kong Triad underlings.

"Hate to sound dense, Smith, but just who is this *you know who* you keep referring to?"

Smith's exasperation escaped like air from a leaking bicycle tire.

"You know as well as I, Petrie, who you know who is whom I'm referring to – whom do you imagine is you know who, if not Fu Manchu!"

I still had enough skag in my blood to avoid gasping with terror. No percentage, anyway. I did cough, less from fear than the dense ganja fog trapped in the Mini.

For years, Weymouth Smith had kept me spellbound with blood-curdling tales of close shaves in the Far East. I had even accompanied him on some dicey missions in Egypt and Laos. The world is clotted up with every sort of evil, and I like to think I've played a small part in thwarting a few varieties of it. But I had never directly contended with the absolute evil that was Dr. Fu Manchu. I'd never even laid eyes on him.

Fu Manchu was the embodiment of evil. The quintessence of evil. The sun and the moon of evil. A one-man axis, or dynamo, of evil. A thousand faces, a thousand personalities. Whole armies of henchpersons, dupes, sycophants, assassins, hypnotized stooges, thugs, grasses, stoolies, puppets – Fu's very name, uttered in some quarters, had been known to induce fatal coronaries in those who'd tasted a mere smidgeon of his implacable wrath.

And Fu Manchu was full of wrath. He was wrath personified. Wrath on a stick. Wrath-mad. Wrathier than a rattlesnake on speed, wrathful in his sinister cunning, wrath-wrapped in his intricate schemes for world domination, the veritable grapes of wrath – skip that, the Supreme Avatar of Wrath.

As for vengeful, you could simply substitute the word *vengeful* for the word *wrath* and get a mere glimmer of his vengefulness.

Now it all made sense. Sort of. Nothing lay beyond the reach of Dr. Fu Manchu's immensely long, tapering fingernails. No human mind was safe from Fu's tamperings. No crime known or unthought of by humankind had gone uncommitted or unattempted by this faceless yet myriad-faced individual, a mastery of cosmetology and prosthetic alternation of the physique and physiognomy. A wizard of mimicry and disguise, with uncountable minions slaking his thirst for power and abetting his designs for global conquest.

And yet an important bit of information wormed its way into my thoughts.

"Smith! It can't be Fu Manchu! He's dead! He died in that

crusher behind the Lotus Blossom Iron Foundry in Ho Chi Minh City!"

"Perhaps," Smith cryptically replied. "But don't forget, Petrie, I've always said that Fu was not the supreme leader of the ChoFatDong, only a high official. In fact, it's often rumored that the real *capo di capi* of the ChoFatDong isn't a man, but woman – a goddess woman, a woman whose diabolism would make Fu Manchu look like a piker."

I pretended to consider this.

"Quite an old woman, I would imagine."

Fu Manchu himself, according to Smith, possessed a longevity serum that had enabled him to see a hundred and fifty winters, at least, come and go.

"Not necessarily. On the contrary. She could be, or at least look like, quite a desirable woman, beautiful and ravishing, who lures victims to their doom by the ChoFatDong with her ethereal, ageless charms."

Anything, alas, is possible.

"At least Fu bought the farm."

Smith's lips coiled into a vexed frown.

"I'm afraid some doubt has surfaced on that score. The Yard, and I, now have the suspicion that what went into that pig iron crusher was one of Fu's blind Mascar slaves, disguised as the impresario of evil. In which case, you know who is just who I suspect he is."

A member of the Air Blaster Gang, one of many tribes of atavists who menaced the streets of London, passed close to the Mini, clutching a Sanjuku Sound Box from which the voice of a long ago songstress, Ethel Merman I believe her name was, momentarily sliced the relatively low street volume. "Life is just a bowl of cherries," warbled the immense, unpleasant voice. "It's so mysterious, it's not serious…"

"All the same, Smith, this doesn't look like the type of restaurant you'd find Fu Manchu in. I mean, this is strictly a moo goo gai pan kind of place."

Smith, his voice weary from decades of peeling veils of illusion from the eyes of others, sounded weary of me, as well: "I doubt if Fu himself is within a thousand miles of here. But his reach is breathing down our very backs. We'll need to start at the bottom of the ChoFatDong food chain and work up. No, Petrie, I don't expect to see Fu in any of his uncountable guises hereabouts. Unless I'm very much mistaken, and I never have been to my knowledge, we should focus for now on these disreputable dog-eating Chinamen. Elsewise, Sir Lionel Parker may become the next victim of the 'Zaybar Kiss.'"

"The Zaybar Kiss – "

"Ask me what it is, and I can only tell you I don't know. But none who have received it has ever lived to tell the tale."

The Zaybar Kiss rang a bell.

Through the aquarium, I saw a fat man squatting at a circular, afromosia teak veneer table, shovelling in the chow like a pig, the way they all do. His enormous face, obscured by the sluggish carp, hardly raised itself from the trough. He looked like the *capo di capi* or whatever you call it of something, a big cheese. A mouldering cheese encased in thick, waxy skin.

His companions wore hyacinth or purple satin jackets with frog-hook buttons. Pigtails ornamented gaudily with varicolored satin bows. An effeminate bunch. The three combined weighed less than their bloated ringleader. I knew how versed in the deadly arts these Oriental pansies can be: killer queens, as Weymouth Smith called them. Their chopsticks lunged mechanically into the carcass of an enormous flounder reposing on a bed of shredded iceberg lettuce.

A refrigeration truck swung up to the curb a few yards in front of us. One of those boxy, aluminum-panelled vehicles used to transport meat from wholesalers to local vendors.

"The Three Dynasties won the Empire through benevolence and lost it through cruelty," remarked Smith. "The wisdom of a bygone age, unfortunately."

He slid a .357 Magnum from his vest pocket and loaded it

from a box of shells in the glove box. Smith slipped out of the Mini before I understood that anything was about to happen.

A fog of green exhaust poured from the chassis of the refrigeration truck.

A fog that bore an alarming resemblance to a mist Smith and I had encountered years earlier in what had once been called Pakistan: Osamaland.

The restaurant entrance visible through glass panels was hidden by red damask curtains. The air felt heavy, syrupy. Smith vanished through the curtains. He reappeared as a scattering of bubbles, as the aquarium filter switched on, lifting the pistol. The chit-chat inside, though I could not hear it, visibly went dead.

A scarlet rosette sprouted on the fat man's forehead. Smith shot the other three as casually as he might have ordered an egg roll. The men had reached into their tunics for weapons, but the element of surprise paralyzed their reflexes. Their heads exploded like squashed melons. Bone and brain matter splattered the fish tank. Some of it landed in the water, where the lobsters and carp instantly began nibbling at it.

As Smith exited, calm as a corpse, he detoured around the refrigeration truck and fired two shots through the windscreen. A spray of arterial blood splashed an exterior side mirror on the driver's side. As Smith passed it, he fired off another bullet.

He yawned as he assumed the wheel of the Mini. Turned the ignition.

"I wonder if I'm not getting eczyma," he pensively remarked as we turned up the access ramp to the motorway. "I itch like the dickens. My legs," he said. "I'll wake up and find I'm scratching my shins with my fingernails. First I thought, bedbugs, you know, or tiny spider bites."

"You might be allergic to some fabric you're wearing."

Signs for Oxmoor and The North flashed overhead.

"It could also be a dietary deficiency."

Smith ruminated.

"We've got to warn Sir Lionel. If I'm not very mistaken, Fu Manchu is either in this country or his emissaries have targeted him for elimination."

"Can't you ring him on your mobile?"

"His lordly mansion is in a dead zone. I hope I didn't give you a shock, killing those five men without warning."

The shot I'd taken had rendered me shockproof.

"I assume they were emissaries of Dr. Fu Manchu."

"They almost certainly were. Especially the fat one. Still, always more where they came from. You know I abhor violence, Petrie. But some people just need killing and that's the long and short of it. God, I itch. I wonder if you could prescribe some sort of ointment or cream."

"I'd have to have a look at the affected area."

The prospect held little allure.

"Perhaps I can show it to you at Sir Lionel's. If we find him alive when we get there. That Zaybar Kiss is always fatal."

"Yes, you mentioned that."

"If you ask me what it is, I can only say I do not know."

It seemed prudent to swallow an anti-loop lozenge, even though Smith did compulsively repeat himself.

5

More reckless driving brought us into the countryside. Pitch black as it was, I sensed the humplike hills and dales, declivities and woodlands, fallow fields and crapulous subsistence farms, the landscape's gentle undulations and cow pastures reminding me of all that is England.

The glorious history of our Nation flashed before my eyes like a ten-second condensation of Masterpiece Theater. Thomas Hardy, for example, hovered in my inner vision in a rotogravure portrait.

I knew that Smith, too, treasured the soil of our ancient heritage. Yet all the great deeds and ancient customs the very name, Britain, summoned in the heart and mind were threatened while England slept, as children tucked up in their beds dreamed whatever children dream, or, sleepless, fingered each other, transfixed by flashlit four-color photographs of spread-open snatch, massive erections, she-males with enormous tits and outdoor plumbing, and for the more fetish-driven… no wonder the country was going to hell in a handbasket.

I pictured torrents of ejaculate spurting into gym socks under percale sheets and comforters, as mums and dads fooled about with their lawfully joined genitalia, oblivious to the diabolism brewing in their own back yards.

Sir Lionel Parker's estate covered several thousand acres

of rolled lawns, primordial forests, babbling brooks, and the like. His home, Cumberfall Mansion, had the appearance of a Rococo lunatic asylum, like a mountain of gingerbread carved into whorling pediments and spires. Towers extruded at its far-flung edges, while embedded along its lower façade were monumental stained-glass windows depicting the imprisonment and beheading of Mary, Queen of Scots, and other noteworthy executions carried out to preserve the Nation.

In such a placid if dreary baronial setting, it was impossible to imagine the darkling cosmos of Fu Manchu: that lurid, insidiously beckoning realm of pachinko parlors and opium dens, of love hotels and miniature condoms, of brothels catering to pedophiles, or eating places where scotties and retrievers roasted on open flames, a world where every vice and depravity flaunted itself.

"I pray I'm mistaken about this," Smith coughed.

"I don't know what you take me for, but you have never in your life prayed for anything, Smith. If you and Fu Manchu have one thing in common, it's your godless view of everything."

Stoned, Smith took the remark in stride.

"Quite so, Petrie. Figure of speech."

"You don't even hope you're mistaken about this, if I know you." If anyone truly knew that complex, perversely dedicated man, it was I. "Let's face it. You're an intrigue junkie. If you weren't, we'd have gotten here hours ago. But no, you needed to rid the earth of a few inconsequent, gibbering chinks."

"They aren't all chinks," Smith said defensively. "I've met a few of the billion or so Chinese who are quite decent."

Lights blazed within the decrepit mansion, as if a seasonal gala were underway. It was not really possible any longer to know what season it happened to be, but Britain adhered to its calendrical customs as a bulwark against anarchy.

"So far," Smith managed to gasp as he drew in the roach-clipped remnant of his spliff, "so good."

We scrambled out of the Mini. Our footsteps crunched on the gravel drive. Under a columned archway, carved oak double doors. They appeared scavenged from an ancient sailing vessel, with a single red light encased in a sort of wrought iron nest overhead. Smith pounded at them ferociously, ignoring the brass doorknocker, sculpted in the shape of a whaling harpoon.

No sound came from within – not at first. I had time to notice the scowling gargoyles carved along the door frames, leering, mocking faces from some anamorphic Hellscape.

The sudden desolation of Cumberfall, despite the riot of light playing upon the stained glass windows, sent icy, premonitory chills through my working veins.

After a prolonged, suspenseful sensation of absolute morbidity within, we heard the distinct shuffling of fluffy carpet slippers.

From behind those fearsome doors came the gruff, irritated howling of an Irishwoman past her prime.

"Who the bloody hell is it pounding out there at this infernal hour?"

Smith recognized the boozy female baritone, apparently, from previous visits to this harsh landscape and its retiring eminence. "It's Inspector Weymouth Smith, Mrs. Murphy! With an urgent message for Sir Lionel!"

The scents of the surrounding forest and a faintly gelid breeze rustling the treetops recalled some moment in the distant past when the word *urgent* had seldom been affixed to anything. I knew we were being observed through a spyhole in one of those gargoyles' eyes, from which a discreet periscope extruded.

The massive doors creaked open.

Before us, as mist began rising from the rolled lawns and enveloping the mansion in a skirt of vapor, a corpulent, large-busted, squinting wreck of a domestic in a quilted housecoat of pink basting and harlequin rhomboids, stolid as a cactus, stood the irascible housekeeper. With, as I'd predicted, furry yellow slippers on her swollen feet. They were shaped like bunny rabbits. Mrs. Murphy herself looked like Lionel Stander in a messy white wig entangled in pink plastic curlers.

"Begorrah, Sir Smith! Why, it's years and listless years for certain since we're privileged with the sight of you at chill and gloomy Cumberfall! And whom, or is it who, that's this ruddy obsequious young figger companioning you like a lamprey through the furtive depths of this brackish night?"

Smith appeared unaccustomed to such fulsome welcome by the hag who drew the ill-fitting housecoat tighter against the stiffening breeze. The red light pooled itself with the jaundiced glow of a chandelier behind Mrs. Murphy's pink curlers.

"Ah, Mrs. Murphy, allow me to introduce my… colleague, Dr. Obregon Petrie. Specialist in internal medicine."

"I wouldn't want such a wee boy poking about inside of me," Mrs. Murphy said, winking lasciviously. "Whereas a man of your stature, Sir Smith – "

Smith cut her off at the pass.

"I'm afraid it's imperative we speak with Sir Lionel without further ado."

But the Murphy creature was having none of it. The aged tart blocked the doorway and struck various poses favoring the full effect of her enormous mammaries, evidently so thrilled to suddenly have the company of two middle-aged male visitors that she imagined herself a sprightly vixen, on the order of Hedy Lamarr.

"Imargin, after sich a Biblical hiatus, buggering yer parden, Sir Smith, how can ye call a word of civil greeting more ado? We've 'ad no ado at all to speak of. Here you turn up in the imperative when we've already settled in on the passive. Not the old slave marster, mind ye – "

She nodded, indicating an area out of visibility.

"My profuse apologies for such perfunctory manners, Mrs. Murphy. You know it's always my heartiest pleasure to see you once again. Alas, my business with the master of the house is pressing."

"Pressing, is it? Well," said she, with a saucy air, "you know Sir Lionel and his nocturnal habits, Sir Smith, one of the wrecks on which civilization is reared, ever up until the hour of the wolf and the midden-scouring raptor, crunching the cinder parth of his grave and wizened mind. Shut up in his study, picking over scarabs and fondling archaeological bric-a-brac scavenged from Egypt and pilfered from Persia, extracting as if reading Braille with his spatulate fingertips the rudiments of vanished eras. Him with his endless arcane speculations about the Hyksos, whatever that is."

"Still a corker, though," winked Smith. "But honestly, we must break in upon Sir Lionel's cogitations – it's a matter of life and death!"

"Life and death!" gasped Mrs. Murphy, aflutter and atwitch. "Blessed Mary Mother of God and Our Lady of Fatima over there in Portugal, why didn't you say so at the outset of your lucubrations?"

She flopped about in carpet slippers on her stout gams, but the overbright entrance hall contained no carpets: only slippery marble tiles which Mrs. Murphy made a game of skimming across after a running start. She collided with yet another pair of oak doors, elaborately hewn with a fiesta of Balinese masks.

"YA GOT RARE COMPANY FOR ONCE, YA MALIN-GERING TYRANT," she barked.

"Hasn't rung for me all night," she confided. "That makes a change. Old fool's always summoning. Looking arfter that one aggravates my piles no end, I hardly mind telling you."

Gripping the door handles, she clearly expected to fling open the awesome portals. They would not budge.

"Now, here's a ripe oddity." The collision had left her breathless, nearly. "Sir Lionel never locks these doors."

Mrs. Murphy now hammered her fists on the oak, with

especial violence where the Balinese masks were carved. Smith followed her example. So did I. From within, not a rustle nor a cough, no peep, nor other sign of habitation echoed.

The housekeeper's prominent eyeballs spun round in their sockets, attempting thought. She stroked a thin moustache below her nose.

"I've got just the thing." Her craggy-visaged inspiration vivified the nexus of capillaries in her booze-ravaged face. "You gents wait right here."

Mrs. Murphy waddled off into the depths of the mansion's bewilderment of corridors. From behind, the harlequin-quilted form resembled a gaudily decorated Mack truck.

Smith chewed his lips, a sure sign of agitation.

"I don't like the looks of this." He spoke whisperingly, as if suspecting hidden microphones.

"I don't like the looks of that treacle tart barging about the premises like influenza, personally. Takes quite a shine to you, doesn't she."

Smith theatrically sighed.

"Mrs. Murphy would take a shine to a platypus, if she thought one would give her a toss. She's repined in this mouldering crypt since the burning of Giordano Bruno, it seems like."

A painting of a public hanging commanded much of the wall near the entrance of Sir Lionel's study. Its artist was unknown to me, but the person swinging from the gallows appeared to date, like the avid crowd watching the festivities, from the period of Newgate Prison's notoriety as a society within a society, the time of Moll Flanders and Jonathan Wild.

I looked closely at every quadrant of this canvas, somewhat Hogarthian in its overall variety of vice-inscribed spectating profiles: the mob alive with twisted faces, malicious eyes, bodies grouped in a manner that indicated a lull in daily hideousness, relieved by the overwhelming lust for the misfortunes of others.

Several minutes passed before we heard a squeaking, creaking, violent dragging noise, punctuated with deep panting breaths and groans. Like the approach of a large exhausted wildebeest.

Mrs. Murphy reappeared, at the terminus of a wide picture-lined hall, pulling and pushing as best she could a square-cut pinewood log that must have weighed over three hundred pounds.

It was an astonishing sight. A ghoulish one, too. Smith, for once, was speechless.

"You gentlemen grab ahold," the crone instructed, and we three positioned the log directly pointed at the juncture of double doors to Sir Lionel's study. We secured armholds on what became, in effect, a battering ram, ripped from the pylons of a rear veranda, according to the housekeeper.

In unison, we backed away about ten steps, then ran the log directly into the study doors. They collapsed inward upon impact, revealing an incredible and incomprehensible scene within.

Mrs. Murphy, taking in the tableau with lengthy bovine confusion, fainted dead away.

6

Here I must relieve my mentor and friend Dr. Petrie of his burden of narrative expatiation. The events of that evening he has thus far described, frenetic and horrible as they were, had their concurrent developments, if I may call them that, at Land's End, and provide salient reason to preempt for a spell Petrie's own dolorous tale.

That the latter might possess some obscure connection with the former was imperceptible at the time, since one hand, so to say, knew not what the other was doing, although I have frequently heard it said that "one hand washes the other."

I have, if I am not mistaken, already described the motley fops and hangers-on for whom Petrie's residence served as a louche gathering place. In his absence its air of desuetude thickened: an atmosphere of crumbling lace, antiquated medical bric-a-brac, the scent of desiccated leather, plates of crumbling cakes, and pots of weak tea prevailed in those dry patches when tubs of Beluga and magnums of Veuve Clicquot did not materialize.

At such fallow times, a muted vibrato of idle anticipation commingled with the presiding ennui, akin to that of a Central European city under foreign occupation. Chez Petrie's specific flavor of intellectual rudderlessness, of dust motes gathering in corners over weeks of nothingness, of slow spiralling clouds of cigarette smoke and melancholy silences, I believe, emanated from an awareness of all who came there that the somnolence and diurnal stillness of Land's End, persistent throughout ten decades, betokened a friable condition of things – which, at an unknowable moment, would no longer remain tenable. That a terrible fracture in the status quo, one day, or more likely one night, would upturn entirely the equilibrium of our peculiarly sedated community.

The first disturbance, for lack of a stronger word, began in the narrow space between the enclosed service area at Colecrupper's Auto Repair and the processional innards of Colecrupper's Car Wash, the latter a cinder block structure through which motor vehicles, their tires mounted on grooved tracks, passed under spinning, barrel-shaped brushes, while floor-mounted jets of industrial cleansers squirted the shells, tires, windows, and under chassis of mulishly advancing cars.

Feculent residue of back road mud, speckles of insecticide the town's pest control biplane deposited everywhere in its twice-monthly overflight, bird droppings, obscenities scrawled in soap across windscreens, and the like were thoroughly slopped by drooling bone-white foam which an overhanging bank of spray hoses then rinsed away.

After the motors passed through these potent baths and sprays and enjoyed the frottage of overhead scrubbers, a platoon of Colecrupper's employees rubbed away all traces of moisture with chamois towelettes and battery-powered hair dryers, leaving glistening, sculpturally eye-catching metal and glass conveyances asquat the customers-only waiting area.

The gap divorcing the two structures, car wash and car repair ports, incarnated a blueprint error incorporated into the otherwise generic design of Colecrupper's Auto Repair and Car Wash: this anomaly had acquired the local appellation "Carwax Alley."

It was an unattended slough where the town's rowdy, glue-sniffing, genetically ill-favored youth gathered after closing. Carwax Alley collected the debris of night, along with the gamey afterscent of rutting: crushed take-out Chinese food containers, shattered styrofoam cups, soggy matchbooks, empty fag packs, used condoms, smashed beer and liquor bottles, the occasional dead rat.

The sole carwash-related function of Carwax Alley was its repository for a battlegreen Dumpster, into which the vacuum-sucked crud from car interiors was discarded. Every other Thursday, a loud, decrepit flatbed truck with metal sides dragged the Dumpster, via clamp-ended metal rods, out of the alley, lifted it over the flatbed of a much-dented yellow garbage truck, flipped it upside down, emptied its contents, then returned it to its original location.

Just before dawn on a Thursday a week before the vernal equinox, the grisly, gut-wrenching discovery in the Dumpster was made, when its foul contents cascaded from its suspended innards, joining a reeking mountain of garbage that Land's End Sanitation had already collected from Pyle, Mockery Hill, and Krapp's Overlook.

The garbage truck operator, Earl Smudge, who derived a tireless, dimwitted pleasure from observing the town's refuse as it tumbled chaotically into his flatbed, at first believed that an inflated rubber dummy, of the type obtained in urban specialty stores, had been discarded into Colecrupper's Dumpster.

It is more than likely, given Earl Smudge's widely discussed personal history, that he conceived some squalid private use for this object, and felt a whelming, then overwhelming impulse to extricate it from the dump heap, with a view, no doubt, towards positioning it mouth-down near the truck's steering wheel as he went about his refuge collection.

It was a typically lusterless morning at Land's End. The evening's revels had subsided long before daybreak. Clouds of a pinkish lavender hue portended a turgid afternoon at sea, and possibly a torrential downpour upon the heedless, sleeping town itself.

The air inert, unpleasantly moist, pungent with the odors

of seabirds, decaying seaweed, and the last bits of a sperm whale stranded by the tide some months earlier – was unusually difficult to breathe.

The serpentine alleys off Gin Lane were noxious with the stench of micturition and upchuck of sailors.

Nowhere could a footfall be heard.

The only sounds anywhere emanated from the closed-on-Thursdays Colecrupper auto service dynasty (Colecrupper was the founder's grandson, and had added the carwash after razing the original service station to the ground, and hiring a so-called architect from Glasgow to give the place what he thought was a Frank Gehry sort of look), namely the grunts and snufflings of Earl Smudge as he slid about knee-deep in refuse and liquefying muck, fiercely struggling to dislodge what he continued to believe, despite growing evidence to the contrary, to be a superbly crafted "love doll."

The object in question, of course, was nothing of the kind. Well, perhaps something of the kind, since the simulacral cooze Earl Smudge had so vividly imagined with instantaneous surmise, in lascivious detail – which his final, agonizing tug, expending Earl's last reliable intake of breath, his troutlike visage contorted by the pulmonary ravages of his midnight amphetamine and emphysema, rattled loose from a garni of disintegrating trash – proved to be the elaborately redecorated corpse of Fanny Bacon: a red-haired, svelte, imprudently accommodating wench-for-hire, whose abnormally large nose preceded her more alluring parts each night into the most disreputable sewers of piratical revelry, catering, it was said, to truly arcane acts of love favored by sailors of far-flung nationalities and ethnic origins deprived for ocean-borne eons of any welcoming orifice attached to a female human.

At sea, men acquire a repertoire of unusual carnal tastes. It would abrogate the timeless code of the seafaring life for them to do otherwise. Nevertheless, the carnal menu served aboard certain Chilean, Peruvian, and Colombian vessels that put in at Land's End every six or seven months, it was said, included more numerous techniques, involving many more body parts and inanimate objects, than might be found aboard the most depravity-pestilent freighters from distant regions of the world.

Surpassing all others in libidinal incontinence (I use the word in every sense cited in the OED), according to sundry chippies of the town, was *The Pamela*, a lighter out of Valparaiso, sailing under Panamanian registry.

Fanny Bacon belonged, or had belonged, to a dwindling claque of our working girls who not only rejoiced whenever *The Pamela* and its alarmingly overendowed, oyster-starved crew was first spotted from the Chatterton Lighthouse on Feral Island (so named for its vast population of cats – often the sole survivors of shipwrecks), but regularly climbed aboard the ship itself when it put in, to welcome these penguinoid Chilean satyrs back to funky old Land's End. Such crews make free with their wages and their lusts for a week before returning to the months of arduous indenture aboard their crafts.

Now, reflected Earl Smudge, Fanny's straddled her last penguin, may she rest in peace.

And, Earl added aloud, may god forgive me for what I am about to do.

The condition in which Fanny Bacon's corpse was uncovered by Smudge, who reported the homicide after parking his garbage truck for several hours off an unpaved road in Hollow Tree Forest, a deciduous wasteland straddling the border line between Land's End and Krapp's Overlook, was unspeakable, and hence the sole topic of conversation at Land's End for several weeks.

I learned of this bestial homicide the following afternoon, at Petrie's house. Petrie encouraged me to make liberal use of his library whenever he was away, scouring the earth for trouble he didn't need with Weymouth Smith. I had drowsily stumbled down to the conservatory, a glass-domed sanctuary for books and exotic plants (Petrie cultivated orchids, among other things, on shelves behind clear mylar sheets), to peruse his first edition of Darwin's *The Descent of Man.*

I never tire of reading Darwin, who wrote what ought to have been the last word on the human species: an aberrant predator, and destroyer of worlds. Other favorites of mine are Fabre's *The Hunting Wasps* and *The Life of the Caterpillar,* as well as that magnificent salute to domesticated animals, *Our Humble Helpers.* And then there is Fabre's irresistible *The Life of the Spider,* which I took from the shelves along with Darwin.

"The Banded Epeira and the Silky Epeira," I read for perhaps the fifteenth time, "those experts in the manufacture of rainproof textures, lay their eggs high up, on brushwood and bramble, without shelter of any kind. The thick material of the wallets is enough to protect the eggs from inclemencies of the winter, especially from damp. The Diadem Epeira, or Cross Spider, needs a cranny for hers, which is contained in a non-waterproof felt. In a heap of stones, well exposed to the sun, she will choose a large slab, to serve as a roof. She lodges her pill underneath it, in the company of the hibernating Snail.

"More often still, she prefers the thick tangle of some dwarf shrub – "

I did not share the literary enthusiasms of Petrie's clique, who read Kropotkin as if he were the Lord Almighty, occasionally switching to Engels, *The Condition of the Working Class in England.*

" – standing eight or nine inches high, and retaining its leaves in winter. In the absence of anything better, a tuft of grass answers the purpose."

The doorbell roused me from the torpid half-sleep I had sunk into while pondering Fabre and the question of whether I ought to return to medical school, or strike out in an entirely new direction. If I didn't settle the question soon, I thought, I shall just go on like this, shunting in my mind between the medical option and some other option, until my options run out. Easy to let fate determine your fate, but then you have to accept what fate doles out. How many times in the previous year had I thought to relocate to Edinburgh, or Manchester, and find a decent speech therapist? Why hadn't I at least taken up some hobby to occupy myself while I waited for inspiration? When in the name of jesus would I get some pussy without having to pay for it?

I rose from the crimson velvet chair beside the faux-Tiffany reading lamp Petrie had been trying to unload on his antiquing customers for years, shuffled into the hall in my blue terry bathrobe, and opened the front doors.

No one was there. Or it seemed no one was there. I scanned the length of Hogg Street for prankish brats, but as the sodden pink clouds still tossed rays of light in their interstices on the asphalt, the presence of children out of doors was unlikely. If some Land's Enders had escaped the grip of daylight lassitude – Petrie and his mates, myself included, were among the immune – virtually none of the town's rug rats stirred before sundown.

I stood in the outer foyer. I stared at the remains of the Burger King at the intersection of Burns Street, all but its signage torched to cinders long ago during one of the town's nocturnal rampages.

Quite near my genitals, something coughed. Glacing down, I saw Thalidomido, the bipolar tyrant of the doll hospital. He wore the garb of a Bavarian mountaineer, including a feathered green hat and matching loden climbing shorts.

His agitation was infectiously urgent. I am allergic to urgency in all its importunate forms.

"I forgot that Petrie was off with that *friend* of his."

Thalidomido gave the word an ironic lilt that wouldn't have surprised me coming from the innkeeper Sauerbrotten, but offended me coming from the dwarf, not that I hadn't already intuited his two-faced nature. How brazen he was in his petty betrayal of Petrie's unstinting hospitality!

Few outside our loose-knit group, I imagine, would have tolerated Thalidomido's mood swings and childishness as long as we had. I assumed he had been having a bad day. He usually did. Yet at Petrie's, he usually painted a jovial face over his travails.

"I have something important to tell him. I suppose I might as well tell you instead."

Some people can never resist the crass urge to let you know you're sloppy seconds.

"Won't you come in," I invited, though Thalidomido had already slipped between my legs into the hall and headed for the drawing room.

Panting as he installed himself in his customary chair near a curio cabinet, he may have run a considerable distance to reach Petrie's house. Thalidomido belonged to the furniture, somehow.

That drawing room, so-called, had been built on a scale no longer practical for our accelerated lives. It more resembled a disused dance hall, though crowded with chairs, sofas, side tables, the circular dining table with a revolving marble inset circle, where we played cards, and the "Cabinets of Wonder" Petrie had acquired at various estate auctions or left by deceased colleagues.

These *Wunderkammer* enclosed an absurd abundance of oddities: Nigerian masks made from animal skins, spirit houses from Central Asia, guardian figures from the Nicobar Islands, linga from India, necklaces made from jaw bones of Brazilian birds; some of Petrie's treasures reposed in sliding shelves, others behind curved glass; even the cabinets themselves were of types no longer made or thought of.

"You seem troubled." I ventured the word hoping he heard it correctly. Without elaborating further, it may've sounded more like "rubbled." The dwarf usually understood my distorted speech, and certainly hadn't expected to find me Hooked on Phonics. Still, when he became *agité*, one could never tell what delusional terrors assailed his disproportionately large head and the disproportionately small brain floating in its broth of blood, tissue, and whatever booze he could get his little hands on, or imagine what other voices sounded like inside that vortex of self-absorption.

"I'm more than troubled." He gulped his port and held out his glass for a refill.

"More than troubled? Whatever has put you in such a state?"

Thalidomido tossed off another port before replying. His profile reflected in a curved cabinet glass, inside which a charm made from a gorilla's skull, its lower jaw absent, was roughly roped to a tibia bone.

Light filtering through the dusty beige curtains filled the air with colorless filaments. I switched on a small chandelier wired to a dimmer, simply to keep objects in that overample, cluttered space slightly distinct.

"It's about Fanny." Thalidomido choked this out in a tragic voice, or as tragic as his high-pitched, squeaky voice could manage.

I knew, though it did not concern me, that Thalidomido had been consulting Petrie on a private basis. Not that Petrie had qualified in psychiatry, but as a medical man he possessed a store of practical wisdom certain patients drew succor from in times of unease.

"Well," I ventured, "I'm afraid I can't help you with anything in the fanny department, old man."

This did not sit well with the dwarf.

"Why does no one make the slightest effort to understand what I mean when I say anything?" he wailed.

He seemed resolved to launch a one-dwarf pity party. As I suffer from an actual speech impediment, his lament caused me a twinge of distaste. He was like the person with no shoes whining to the person with no feet. (I am, in order not to slow my narrative to a crawl, rendering my own speech into ordinary English.)

"What I meant was," I said gently, "if it's fanny you're having a bumpy time with, I'm no expert in the wiles and wherefores of the female of the species."

Thalidomido almost sprayed out his mouthful of port.

"Dead, dead." He spat the word. "Fanny! Dead! All over the place!"

This, parenthetically, looking back on it, had proven not quite accurate. The woman I continued to mistake for a vulgar common noun at the time had not been dismembered and strewn about, but merely eviscerated, stabbed, and strangled, though none of us would know all the details until the coroner's report became public.

"Most fanny hereabouts is pretty dead," I conceded. "But let's not go overboard. They don't all watch the clock and yawn while you're pumping away. Don't let one disappointing rendezvous completely color your outlook."

No comeback. I resented his presence, as it forced me to say something, anything, to fill the petulant silence.

"You know," I said, each word somehow swelling up from the last, like bubbles on a bar of hand soap, "I bet you anything, if you tipped them a little better, you'd get plenty of life back into their snatches. Excuse me for saying so, but you do have a reputation for parsimony."

His demeanor now suggested the onset of an epileptic seizure. I wondered if dwarves ran a statistically higher risk of epilepsy than the common run of humankind.

"You idiot." His voice dripped with disgust. I might add that Thalidomido's own voice had considerably less sonority than Richard Burton's. It squealed and squeaked like a child's, and somehow being called an idiot by such a cretin caused me to burst out laughing. But here was one pot that never hesitated to call the kettle black. Raised by wolves, I rather thought.

To be completely candid, I could barely stand this Napoleonic runt from some carny barker's litter, and often had felt tempted to kick him across the room with one of my size 12s. If I'd refrained, it was merely to avoid drawing attention to my person, and with the others absent, the urge was all but irresistible.

I stood up from the card table where I sat several feet from him, stretched, yawned, and performed that neck-bending exercise where you rotate your topmost vertebrae by rolling your head left to right, right to left, then drop your shoulders; I casually crossed the room in retreat, glancing with boredom at the high ceiling, straightened a candelabra, then stood at a three-panelled window, staring out as I smoked a cigarette.

All my silent padding about had the intended effect. "You aren't king of anything around here," I didn't need to say aloud. "See how big this room is? Look like a doll hospital to you?" Finally, it sank in that I was not one of his "little people" braceros enduring his gripes.

I can only guess what his thoughts were, if he had some, but a cautious look came over his face, as if he only then perceived that we were utterly alone. I could toss him out by the seat of his climbing shorts with complete impunity.

Contrite or simply scared, he changed his tune.

"Good grief. Why did I say such a cruel thing? I implore your forgiveness, old friend. I'm all on edge. I hardly know what I'm saying. I've also been getting this incredibly irritating itch on my arms and legs. Like little bugs underneath my skin."

I moved closer to his chair.

"Of course I forgive you, but why take it out on me?" I decided to give him a taste of his own back. "Colecrupper's the one who's always shooting you the evil eye, not me."

"I never noticed that." He pondered. "Though it doesn't surprise me, really. That time he was so puffed up with himself, when he finished reading *The Eighteenth Brumaire of Louis Bonaparte.* Of course it took him six months to get through it, if he really did."

"That's because all Colly Colecrupper does at home," I said, falling into gossip mode, "is weave those ridiculous Honduran baskets. He's never sold a one. That, and… wrestles with his bad conscience."

A look of normal amazement restored Thalidomido's appetite for backbiting, which invariably trumped his melancholia.

"You mean about Judy?"

He shot me an apologetic, self-directed scowl, disgusted that he couldn't resist jumping up and waddling to the vodka bottle.

"But… but that's more than twenty years ago! And if you ask me, it wasn't such an acrimonious split up. She had her clothing line and then her uncle – no, her aunt, left her all the money, didn't she?"

"Her Aunt Thelma, I think Petrie once told me."

"Thelma." Thalidomido uttered the name dreamily. "That's a name I haven't heard mentioned in years. You're far too young to have known her, but you'd be in for a real treat if she were still around. She turned that cramped little bakery over on Tannhauser Lane into a whole grain empire. Erna Cuntze set her up in business. That was before Erna fell under the spell of that slob she married. What a shrewd mind that Thelma had, ticking away under all the Biba lipstick and silver Egyptian kohl! I can still see Thelma St. Albin in the heyday of her allure."

"Well, I take it she left the bread business investments to Judy. Petrie witnessed the will, so he should know."

"Judy still has the cheekbones. Last time I went down to London I looked her up. I know Thelma was only an aunt, but she inherited Thelma's eye for the main chance, that's for sure."

We were back on safe terrain. For the time being.

"What I've never figured out," I quizzed, "is why the fuck she ever married Colly in the first place."

Thalidomido shrugged emphatically.

"He still just basket weaves and mopes about Judy? My god, he really has no inner life, does he?"

"I don't know when you last took a focused look at Colly Colecrupper," I said, "but, not to be catty, he hasn't got much outer life, either."

As in any social microcosm, our little group gathered around Dr. Petrie had its internecine tensions. Stresses, aversions, mannerisms that worked one another's nerves.

This talk of inner and outer life, alas, sank Thalidomido back into doom and gloom. His real problem, I thought, was drinking all the time on top of lithium. That combo will probably kill a dwarf even faster than a taller person. I felt the vodka myself, and had a vague wish to go outside.

"I really lost my composure, saying what I did to you."

"Oh, forget it. Please. I do act like an idiot, when an idiotic mood comes over me. None of us is perfect. I mean, maybe someone is, how would I know, but nobody I've recently met."

The afternoon light was paling, brightening the chandelier and its warm burnish of dusty surfaces and smudged cabinet glass. I did the best I could to keep Petrie's salon a bit less sullen-looking, but even Glass Wax and Lemon Pledge left it looking like a museum piece, something under a bell jar.

"You really are a sensitive soul, aren't you? I really don't understand myself, I'm a wreck. I take those suppositories every day like clockwork and I still get all… whatever. So much tension at the Palace of Dwarves. So many shattered dolls…"

Thalidomido lurched forward on his cane-backed throne, cupping his glass, now a picture of earnestness copied from an Ealing Studios B production of the 1940s.

"Every time I look at one, I feel like a broken doll myself. You can't imagine what it's like, working with a bunch of 'little people' all day. They may look little on the outside, but they can be a giant pain in the rectum. Your very being feels diminished.

62

Your perspective dwindles. And now these, you know, deformed midgets we hired to cope with those Sharia Law Barbies the company should have recalled the minute they bombed Selfridges. They're edging out my applicants. Not that I'm getting any. So now the authentic dwarves, one by one, they're giving notice.

"These new hires… something sinister about them. They don't come right out and claim to be dwarves and you can tell the difference from their heads, they've got a whole different chromosome arrangement. Don't interpret this the wrong way, because it's not about… I've had plenty of friends who were midgets. We still have a few dwarves on staff, but one's just given notice, and I doubt that Fernando sees gluing arms and legs and miniature wigs on little lumps of plastic as a ticket to ride anywhere special. He'll leave me. All the competent ones do."

I nodded understandingly, though of course I didn't understand a word he said. Labor relations are not my forte. Fernando, I seemed to recall, was a swarthy Armenian who had cuckolded every male employee at the doll hospital at one time or another. Somehow they always forgave him. Perhaps they grabbed some action from that quarter now and then themselves. As for Thalidomido and his staffing complaints, I couldn't really put myself in his shoes. They were far too small. A heterosexual drama queen really shouldn't be a dwarf on top of everything else.

"Before, what I was trying to say about Fanny – I meant Fanny Bacon. She's dead!"

"The whore?"

Thalidomido sniffled and broke down.

"Fanny was more than just a whore to me." He blew his nose between his fingers and regained his composure.

Another good piece of ass down the drain, I thought. I really must stop wavering about medical school, flee this torporville, get started on something constructive while I still have a bit of my youth left. But Thalidomido wasn't finished.

"It may surprise you to hear this, but... my junk down there is normal size. Fanny always told me it was even bigger and thicker than average. Of course, she might just have said that out of kindness, but I've measured it fully erect, and – "

I cut him off quickly.

"But this is dreadful. Everyone loves Fanny. Loved Fanny, I should say. Had she been ill?"

It was true, Fanny was a local favorite. Even I had loved Fanny for an hour and fifteen minutes not more than sixteen months before her passing. I remembered to that day how firm her clam muscles were. They had clamped my substantial, uncircumcised member in a silken grip tighter than any I had previously known.

"Well, somebody didn't love her, because she was *murdered*."

Shocking news summons the strangest thoughts. I caught myself wondering if the perpetrator of this crime had perhaps loved Fanny too, in his own way, perhaps after killing her rather than before. Earl, of course, prior to hanging himself six months later, wrote a letter confessing his own one-off with the posthumous Fanny. He had added, tastelessly in my view, that the miracle of that interlude had been that, even in death, Fanny had been "still tight." Rigor mortis, more likely, but how would a degenerate like Earl know the difference?

On the other hand, the rest of Earl's letter contained several moving passages in which he revealed a fulsome appreciation of the complete pointlessness of his existence without a trace of self-pity. *I chose this life of filth*, Earl had written somewhere in his verbose but interesting suicide note. *To wallow in garbage, to smell all the time of other people's crap, to waste all the days at my disposal – no pun intended – moving around the same rut, from one pile of waste matter to the next, without the slightest variation, like a rat in a maze, a stinking worthless genetic mistake, living in a crumbling caravan as filthy as my flatbed at the end of a long day, laying around drunk watching pornographic videos of interracial three-ways and jerking off, I could have changed it all at any time but nothing doing, I've never had an ounce of initiative or stuck to any project I started longer than it took to empty that Dumpster of Colecrupper's, I hope I don't fuck up my suicide the way I fucked up everything else.*

To Earl's credit, his suicide had been an uncharacteristic success in every way. That's all I can recall at the moment. Poor Earl. I wish I could remember anything positive, or even anything negative, to record about him here, but we seldom appreciate the emptiness of other people's lives until they've left this vale of tears and unpleasant odors, and usually, or at least such is my experience, we forget all about them the minute they're gone. Unless, like Earl's farewell missive, they leave something behind to remember them by.

Who can say? Perhaps Earl's memory will live on, simply because of one session of necrophilia with a butchered whore and a suicide note the length of a John Updike story in *The New Yorker*. And what does it matter now to Earl, or to me, or to you?

Thalidomido, meanwhile, was in tears. Mood stabilizers and booze, a must to avoid. Bullies are all crybabies under the skin anyway, as everybody knows. Psychos murder whores right and left every minute of the day, it's sad, but that's the way of the world. I'd prefer that an entirely different category of persons were the ones who got murdered that often, but if wishes were horses, et cetera.

The brief impulse to console Thalidomido with a fortifying hug quickly passed, either because I found physical contact with him a repugnant prospect, or because, at that moment, Philidor Wellbutrin, glorified abortionist (as I privately thought of him), burst into the drawing room.

"Good grief," Wellbutrin exclaimed without preamble. As he did so, he broke wind loudly – fortunately, downwind from myself. "You won't believe what's just happened. I've just lost one of my best patients to some homicidal maniac. A nice girl, too. She came every week to make sure the visiting rowdies hadn't given her clap or something worse. And I happen to know she never missed morning mass, seven mornings every week of her life."

"I didn't know you were Catholic." I couldn't think what else to say.

"I'm not, but all the same. Don't you wish there were a god who'd take her spirit up to paradise?"

Up quark, down quark, neutrons: that is all the physical universe consists of, yet Wellbutrin persisted in thinking something perishable goes "up" when it perishes. Strange.

"If you can tell me where her spirit is right now, Dr. Wellbutrin, I'll take it to the movies with me." Any mention of god raises my cackles, or whatever they're called. I knew our one decent cinema, The Proxy Bijoux, was screening a double feature: *It Happened One Night* with *A Night to Remember*.

Wellbutrin lunged for a bottle of Curaçao on the wheeled liquor bar.

"Nasty way for anyone to finish up, all the same," he mused, pouring vodka on top of the blue liqueur.

He examined the rim of his glass and sighted the dwarf, the gorilla skull, the dust motes in the chandelier's dim light.

I stood up again, idly rotating the marble inset of the card table.

"How did she finish up, exactly? That one there has been a weeping willow since he slithered in and he still hasn't told me."

"They found her in the Dumpster in Carwax Alley. Her throat practically ripped out, with puncture wounds all over her body. Someone took a scalpel to her torso as well. It reminds me of a Korean horror movie I rented the other day. Can't remember the title. The guy in that was taking off women's faces and then he'd dissolve their whole bodies with some solvent.

Not even teeth remaining. At first, the detectives thought – oh, I've forgotten now what they thought, but finally, one of them realizes that he does the whole body because he doesn't want it discovered *what was wrong with the victim's heart* – because the killer takes the hearts out, see. And sells them to this transplant doctor. There's some kind of AB-negative angle involved, but the guy kills the doctor before they can question him again. Really good acting in that one.

Fanny, though, whoever did this didn't take anything out… no internal organs or what have you. No useable parts. It's shocking when it happens in real life. I don't think anything like this has ever happened in Land's End."

Thalidomido appeared poised to dispute the assertion, but instead silently splashed more vodka into his tumbler.

Earl also confessed to returning Fanny's body to where he had found it. It began to haunt him, he wrote, almost immediately afterwards, that since he'd emptied the Dumpster, she would now be truly alone, without even the consolation of garbage. What he'd told the police was that he'd lost his signature tam o'shanter – probably the only way anyone ever recognized him besides the stench he gave off – gone back to Colecrupper's in case it had slid off his head while wheeling the Dumpster back into place, and only then found Fanny inside it.

This ineptly improvised fib mucked up the timeline of the Fanny Bacon investigation, another thing Earl Smudge expressed remorse over in his suicide note, if you can call a fifteen-page exegesis of a lifetime in small, compressed handwriting a note. I have a xerox copy of Earl's note, made from a copy Petrie received when he returned, months later, to Land's End.

I might've stopped the other killings if I hadn't been thinking with my dick as per usual, Earl wrote. Being dead, he would never learn that nothing would have stopped the other killings, least of all anything Earl Smudge did or didn't do.

Officially our medical examiner, Petrie had finessed a part-time salary for a retired back-up coroner to cover for him when he travelled. A retired croaker name of Crashnitz, living in Pyle with an alleged pediatric nurse name of Mavis. Tits that would give a twelve-year-old a coronary. I had happened to be present on their single visit to Petrie's home: quite a team.

According to Wellbutrin, Crashnitz had raised a real stink about not being summoned to the scene until several hours after Earl reported his "discovery" of Fanny's corpse. Ironically, given Wellbutrin's synopsis of the film he'd rented, Crashnitz had been furious that all of Fanny's transplantable parts had run well past their expiration date by the time he got there.

"Odd burk, that Crashnitz," Wellbutrin added. "And that *Mavis*! What sensational breasts!"

His need for another stiff drink screamed from every pore. Thalidomido's sobs became a torrent of lachrymose, nauseating self-display. I, too, badly craved the obliteration of alcohol.

As I adumbrated earlier, Fanny Bacon's killing was but one of the disturbances that began to pester Land's End. I might add that, horrible as it was, it proved far from the most spectacular and brutal event in the sequence. Before relating these happenings that shattered the town's century-long stasis, I must return this account to Petrie's narrative, as it appears I have left that in abeyance overlong.

7

"Bleeding fucking christ, Petrie!"

Smith reeled at the scene of mayhem that confronted us after smashing in the doors of Sir Lionel Parker's study.

I, dumbfounded, surveyed an incomprehensible *tableau morte*. Massive bookcases had been hurled over, vitrines of archaeological specimens smashed and looted, an enormous revolving globe in an elaborately carved wooden plinth now lay athwart a shattered glass vitrine, the globe itself spattered with blood. Everywhere, like snowflakes, ripped-up paper shards, bearing Sir Lionel's distinctive, left-tilted handwriting. They littered the Bokhara carpet, the plush chairs where Sir Lionel seated his visitors, and the wreckage evident in every part of that once-sedate room.

A small mummy case, evidently the final repository of an extremely small Pharaoh, had been jammed into the fireplace, where it smouldered like a huge chunk of anthracite.

This shrieking vandalism, I hasten to add, was far from the most shocking sight in that study. For, in what I may as well term the epicenter of the doleful scene, illumined by a bookkeeper's lamp hooded in green glass, stood Sir Lionel Parker's sturdy teakwood desk, its surface naked of all objects except a small puzzle-patterned carved box inlaid with agate and turquoise formica, while behind the desk, in the venerable oxblood leather chair Sir Lionel occupied whilst pursuing his formidable researches… sat, or in some manner reposed, in a wildly unnatural position, a… thing, enveloped in Sir Lionel's own signature silk embroidered robe, eau de Nile in color… an entity, or organism, somehow suggestive of Sir Lionel himself, in an evanescent, grossly distorted manner. This thing was not, on cursory appraisal, Sir Lionel himself, but a pale, segmented, human-scaled… *insect larva*!

The larva, like some taunting effigy, was wearing Sir Lionel's school tie, as well as his robe, and, in several places along its milky epidermis, if I may call it that, had emerged… *appendages*, resembling the legs of an impossibly gigantic arachnid. One such rested on the gleaming desktop in a parody of a scholar's hand, fisted at rest between bouts of literary composition. A slip of folded lavender paper under this frightful extremity caught my attention.

This creature, whatever it was, had the unmistakable look and smell of partial decomposition. Its mozzarella-colored flesh bore patches of lividity, and its antennae (yes, ghastly to recount, it had two stalklike extrusions at its oily apex, presumably its "head") limply drooped against what I am still hesitant to call its "face," though I knew, as I felt certain Smith had discerned before I, that the glabrous, uninfected tissue covering the monstrosity's topmost segment had, until quite recently, been the saturnine, finely chiselled face of Sir Lionel Parker.

Despite the inward revulsion and grief he must have suffered like the blow of a fireplace poker to his cranium, Smith remained ever-watchful, insistent that nothing in the room be touched, lest some important clue be muddied, or a still-lurking menace cause one or both of us to meet Sir Lionel's apparent fate. He approached the desk with the soundless tread of a Himalayan cat, his eyes on the inlaid box and the note that clawlike limb pinned to the desk.

He now turned businesslike on a dime. Such was his keen,

blunt-sharpened mind that I knew he'd scented clues already. He revealed nothing about these clues in order to acquire enough of them to astonish me with the breadth of his deductive skill. This exercise in mild sadism came with the territory. Smith had to let you know how much smarter than you he was. I wasn't his first Boswell-Watson, and I would not be the last. In recent times, Smith's habitual pushiness had so often threatened to separate me from a reliable opiate source that a parting of ways no longer seemed unthinkable. Still, whenever he called, I came running like a poodle.

Frankly, I would've gone anywhere to get away from Land's End.

Smith gingerly extracted the lavender square from beneath the claw, as I guess you'd have to call it, of the moribund larva that had once been Sir Lionel Parker. He cautiously sniffed at it, unfolded its origami creases, again surveyed the demolished study, and at last handed it to me.

It bore a scrawled message, possibly made with crayon.

> *Made you look, you dirty crook*
> *I considered hatching this senile embryo, but changed my mind.*
> *Jamais, jamais de ma vie…*
>   *You know who*

"Who does this foul intruder think he is, Édith Piaf?"

Smith's grimace told me he knew more, far more than I did.

"Petrie, only one person could or would have written this taunting dare to find him. I don't claim he wrote it personally. In all likelihood, he dictated it to one of his mind-slaves. Note that it says '*ma vie*' rather than '*la vie.*' As usual, it's all about him."

I had prudently brought along my loop lozenges, but somehow knew I didn't need them.

"As you know, Dr. Fu Manchu, who possesses the prominent brow of a Shakespeare, the most brilliant scientific mind the world has ever known, the fingernails of Nosferatu, and a psyche deranged enough to make Daniel Paul Schreber look like the *ne plus ultra* of mental health, has devised a super high-pitched signal that reduces everything in its range to its constituent molecules.

"Fortunately for our world, the thing doesn't work. Yet. It's a little… saucer contraption shaped like a kitchen appliance, or it was, anyway, when I glimpsed it once in Manitoba, Canada, of all places. I do know for a fact he's always fiddling with the design. Fu Manchu has boasted of being the world's greatest appliance designer in addition to his other preternatural abilities, but has yet to prove it. He's missing a vital element for this deadly device, and has been combing the earth with his minions of darkness in search of it. For, of course, purposes of world domination, his primary goal, the ultimate focus of his machinations. Fu has been pissed about having to look for this stuff since Formosa turned into Taiwan."

I stared at the blood spatter pattern on the overturned globe when a voice interrupted our silent meditations. *"You know perfectly well, Weymouth Smith, that I am one of the world's few scientific geniuses – perhaps the greatest scientific genius of all time, that I have the mind of five scientific geniuses rolled into one…"*

"Creepy to hear this madman throwing his voice around from who knows where," Smith whispered near my ear. "But I suspect, given the slight crackle in his diction and his tedious repetition of the phrase 'scientific genius,' that what we're hearing is a pre-recorded subterfuge. If I'm correct, Dr. Fu Manchu is long gone from Cumberfall Mansion, if indeed he personally was ever here. Incidentally, there are other things scattered in this room that point to an elaborate scheme to introduce a pathogenic gas into this study."

"Could that be the Zaybar Kiss?" I ploddingly asked, thinking that it couldn't.

"Far from it, Petrie. Far from it. What I fear we're dealing with here makes the Zaybar Kiss look like heavy petting. In only one place on earth have I heard of evidence of this... de-speciesification of a human entity. We're about to do some rough travelling, Petrie. To Northwest Guyana, to be precise."

"You mean in the highlands of the Orinoco region?"

"Not *necessarily* the highlands, though that's a fair guess. But a fair number of cataracts, gorges, cliffs, and poisonous reptiles exist in the area, and the night-blooming flower no person who sees it dares ever to name. It's a myth that there are no fields and pastures there, FYI. One finds them at peculiar elevations. It's a putrid country, crawling with lowlifes and souvenir vendors, and one I'd gladly avoid if that were possible. Strange things occur there, Petrie. Terrible things. But there is no other way."

We both looked weary as lint, I'm sure, and Smith was too tired to explicate, myself too bored to listen to the process by which he'd reached his deduction. My personal needs were making themselves felt.

As if in tandem, we became aware of yet another unnatural aspect of the night's events.

You'll recall that moments after storming Sir Lionel's chamber, Mrs. Murphy succumbed to a swoon or faint, dropping to the chessboard marble tiles outside the study. Her hammy legs, if I've neglected to mention them, by happenstance had been visible spread-eagled in the doorway, in the unintended attitude of a common streetwalker impatient to commence and more or less simultaneously include the act of jiggy-jiggy and quickly collect her swag. Naturally there was a more innocent reason for Mrs. Murphy's deshabille, an innocence one would assume, in any case, since even a novice prostitute worth her salt not only carries Mace but demands full fee in advance.

As we again moved cautiously among the cyclonic damage, it dawned on me that this horror had to have been a long, nasty, noisy job, well within the hearing of the far-from-deaf Mrs. Murphy.

I had ignored this thought when it first arose, still absorbing the grotesquerie in front of my face – the dire metamorphosis of Sir Lionel and the mephitic odor of what would now, I ventured to suppose, properly be called the former Sir Lionel, if I may speak of him thus, or rather the sulphurous fumes exuded by his… *egg casing*, as the tiered blobs of tissue appeared to be, or else the natural odor of the implausibly gargantuan spider or what have you that expired as it attempted emergence from its cocoon, and of course the Hesperus-like wreckage of the study that lay everywhere about us, added to the likelihood that Sir Lionel Parker's lifework had been obliterated and lost to posterity.

In short, neither of us had given the old slag who let us in a second thought while pruning through ripped and shredded residua, amid which the magnum opus Sir Lionel had labored upon for decades was now a ubiquitous confetti, impossible to piece together.

But I now sensed, even before my eyes confirmed, that the garrulous Irishwoman who'd been prostrate as mangled roadkill only minutes before had vanished.

"Smith," I whispered, in case the diabolical assailant, his penchant for theatrical carnage unassuaged by transforming the pacific master of Cumberfall into some manner of segmented worm, or spider, or nightcrawling translucent bug, or one of Fu Manchu's unspeakable "genetic hybrids," lingered about in a strange form or other. Those things sticking out of Sir Lionel's flesh casing bore a distinct resemblance to a creature Smith had once described, I recalled, as "a sort of amphibious lobster whose legs and feelers shrink to resemble the limbs of its arachnid cousins when the things have been out of water a while."

Smith exchanged knowing glances with me. We rushed into the hall.

The hefty beam we'd used to bash in the doors, in the strong light of the chandeliers, looked wormy, and, if one can say such a thing about a log of wood, exhausted from its efforts.

In the same corridor where Mrs. Murphy had dragged forth the wormy lumber, the lights dimmed, but only, it appeared, to highlight objects strewn on the glistening marble, directly under small halogen puddles of track lighting.

This twilight atmosphere summoned unwelcome, half-erased memories of the distant past. Fiona. A nocturnal hunt for Easter eggs in a garden maze. Somber emotions flushed through me like a bowel movement through a W.C.'s waste pipes.

The first things we came upon were Mrs. Murphy's breasts. Those seeming wonders of nature now revealed the handiwork of a skilled manufacturer, packed with sacs of animal fat, their nipples bosky and large as Chinese luck coins, aureoles ringed with miniscule bumps.

Following a trail that mocked us at every step, we discovered more: Mrs. Murphy's synthetic vagina, embedded between prosthetic upper thighs. Her cunt hair was shaved and dyed into a rude lower-body Mohawk buzz-cut.

The buttocks of whatever creature had so convincingly impersonated Sir Lionel's lusty housekeeper had been separated and placed under two engravings in ormolu frames, facing each other from opposite walls. These were reproductions from Goya's *Caprichos*: at left, *Aquellos polbos*, or *This Dust*, depicting a witch trial, the defendant wearing a vertiginous dunce cap; at right, *A caza de dientes*, or *Out Hunting for Teeth*, in which a woman protecting her face with a cloth reaches into the open mouth of a hanged man to wrench with her fingers a good-luck tooth. The right buttock lay face-up, so to speak, beneath the latter, the left a sculptural footnote to the former.

Further along the corridor, looking more hastily discarded than her lady parts, the faux Mrs. Murphy's fuzzy bunny slippers protruded from her now empty harlequin housecoat. Their silly bunny faces now were part and parcel of the intricate atrocity

Dr. Fu Manchu had contrived in his never-ending attempt to induce a nervous breakdown in Weymouth Smith, an effort, as I knew from Smith's recounting of his earlier scrapes with the Oriental master criminal, was second only to world domination on Fu's list of things to make and do.

The pseudo-Murphy's hair, or rather wig, still enmeshed in a ganglia of snap-on plastic curlers, dangled from a bridge lamp illuminating a large reproduction of Velasquez's *The Surrender of Breda.*

"All points to an Hispanic theme. Guyana. The kanaimà."

Smith, when avid, spoke telegraphically.

The actual Mrs. Murphy took us hours to locate, bound, gagged, and extremely deceased behind a Weiner Werkstätte commode in a second-story storage room. She had expired at least a week before, roughly estimating time of death from olfactory foulness and visible decomposition. The former housekeeper had putrefied in the body cavities. Lividity had set in somewhat faster than I'd have expected, given room temperature and the almost airless space she'd been jammed into. I could find no evidence of insect depredation, surprising in a house this porous, and ligature marks in the throat area.

"Cause of death, Petrie?"

"We'd need a full autopsy."

"No time for that. A full forensic examination could hold us up for days. For all we know, that's all the time Fu Manchu needs to destroy Western civilization."

"Learning the cause of death might indicate something."

"All it would indicate is what she died of, not how this rabid dog of a genius chink is planning to kill us all."

"What if the person we thought was Mrs. Murphy was actually Fu Manchu herself, I mean himself?"

Smith gave this short shrift. Lit his pipe, packed with ganja.

"Possible. Can mimic any voice. Assume any guise. And, since last October, when the iMe came on the market, or for that matter using a blowgun and a loop needle, he could've done a walk-in on the real Mrs. Murphy, and had her transform Sir Lionel into a great big aphid or whatever, though he obviously chose otherwise, since she was long gone before Sir Lionel was, by the smell of things. When faced with innumerable possibilities, Petrie, the wisest course is to eliminate all of them."

We had gone outside the storage room for whatever fresh air could be had in the drafty hall.

"But that leaves us with nothing," I protested.

"*Au contraire*," Smith puffed. "Our nemesis is taunting us. Defying us to find him. Yet leaving a conspicuous hint that will lead us to him."

Down the rabbit hole again, I thought. I badly needed to fix up.

"He sounds like a split personality. What hint?"

"The breasts. The vagina with the magenta Mohawk. The wig on the lamp. You noticed what kind of lamp it is?"

"Please, Smith, I've been peddling antiques between shipments of H for years now. I know a bridge lamp when I see one."

He's going to bait me at a time like this, I thought. He can't help himself. I can't help myself. No one can help anything.

"Do you know where dismemberment and the scattering of body parts, in exactly the configuration we confronted in the hall, and the transformation of one's enemy into a giant bug, has been a ritual of retribution for the past three hundred years? Do you know that the accursed place I'm referring to is within a hundred yards of a primitive rope and plank affair over a thousand-foot chasm known as the Green Bridge, or Long Fall Down?"

I didn't know. I didn't care. I knew what a long fall down was, I'll say that much. The Green Bridge was a piker compared with what I'd taken.

We were back in the foyer. We walked on the roiling fog.

"If you insist on playing twenty questions, Smith, it's my turn to go first: do you know where I can pass a script for Dilaudid at this hour, anywhere within a hundred kilometers of this rural pisshole? Because if you don't, no way in Hades am I going up the Amazon or down the falls at Iguazú or cross the fucking River Jordan, or whatever life-threatening jaunt you have in mind *and* going through withdrawal at the same time. I swear the moment you get an idea fixed in mind it lodges there like some bloody sewer pipe against all reason and squirts any alternatives out through your ears."

I hear my voice. I hear his voice. I can imagine our voices tangled up like a wad of rubber bands, crackling of bubblewrap stomped by an angry god, my spine snapped in half, time itself leering at me, memories torn from my brain matter.

"Petrie, get hold of yourself, don't you think it's imperative to stop Fu Manchu? Would I have intruded on your seaside decrepitude if I thought I could stop him all on my lonesome?"

Stop him from *what*? my brain screams. Stop him from putting a period on this interminable sentence, stop him from releasing us from the bonds of earth. Stop what?

"I think it's imperative I hit a working vein with a full syringe in the next half-hour, or for all I give a shit, Fu Manchu can dominate the planet and turn it into random molecules and eat it, too."

Need. All this need, all this fog, this damp.

All we do is argue. Argue and play games. I felt myself turning into a giant aphid.

"I want to go back to Land's End." I felt like Jane Wyman in an access of wan but accepting disappointment. Why keep this up. Why.

"I just hate myself when I get so domineering," Smith was saying. Now, I thought. Now come the *I'm sorrys* I've listened to a million times. "My nerves are shot. I'd never ask you to disrupt your life and risk your neck in the hell of northwest Guyana without having enough junk to get you there. We'll book a stopover in Caracas. I'm sure we can find a writing doctor in a city that size. If worse comes to worst, I'll pay a visit to my Latino colleagues at Interpol or some police impound. You can't hit a better score than an impound. All they keep in them are dope and weapons. We'll need both, probably."

The worst was, deep down, I knew I'd never met anyone remotely as interesting as Weymouth Smith. After all the sordid shit he'd dragged me into, I still found the Ahab in Weymouth more entertaining than the Uriah Heeps of my clientele, the recidivist syphilitics and low-rent junkies, and those humiliating Christmas gigs at the antique store.

I rolled up my sleeve as I slid into the passenger side of the Mini. Instantly Smith eased a hospital-quality spike into the vein in the crook of my elbow: my favorite. We were friends again.

8

As the Boeing 767 sliced through clouds shaped like plumes and polar bears, giant ducks and hog intestines forming and reforming from cottony strands of impacted moisture, others abscessed by bruise-green refractions from the seawater and the Miniature Simulated Rainforest Wonderland Park on Tristan da Cunha miles below, I wished I'd kept the vodka in my carry-on. The aircraft really did seem to ingest time and space rather than pass through it.

The plane's obsolescent section screens showed different films, in different sections. As it hurled itself towards Caracas I drifted in and out of a feeling of inhabiting the plane and occupying empty space, while Smith aimed his concentration on a book with yellowing pages and engraved illustrations. I felt too wasted to note what the images looked like. My eyelids kept dropping like phospheme-emblazoned opera curtains over my retinas and I abandoned myself to nothingness, my final conscious thought being that I had no idea where to score dope in Venezuela. But being a doctor, this didn't keep me awake. The impound idea seemed promising.

I dreamed in little jolts of imagery that must have been the tamed effects of much larger and alarming people or events in the waking world. The narrows of wakefulness revealed the face of Justin Timberlake on the film running on the seat in front of me. Always shot in ¾ profile, with a closely trimmed beard, more like a pencil stroke.

"Come to me, Petrie."

A Eurasian girl? She wore the sheerest of white veils, beckoned from the entrance of a seraglio or a rug merchant's emporium. Was she real? Did she exist? Are these two versions of the same question?

"If anyone asks, we're down here consulting on the Escobar Lombarto investigation in Bolivia, this is just a stopover."

He is speaking to me, from a cosmic distance, turning a crumbling page of his illuminated manuscript. I merge with the image.

"But we're not investigating the Escobar Lombarto killings. I don't even know what they are."

"Then how can you be certain?"

The plastic shell of the airliner, the essence of cheapness, ugliness, discomfort.

"Because I took Logic in school, Smith. What could these atrocities in Guyana have to do with Lombarto Whatsis?"

Killing and fucking. What else real do people do.

"Absolutely nothing. But consider this: all matter is connected in some way or another. We, for example, are now landing in Caracas. They've lowered the landing gear. Now we see the earth below the cloudline, currents of water, land. Only seconds ago, we were thousands of feet higher up, in an atmosphere of dense clouds."

I nodded: what else could you do with Smith? He spared me whatever astounding insight he'd had concerning the connection of all matter in the universe, as his voice was eclipsed by the screech of the plane's tires skidding on tarmac.

Inside the terminal, a wiry man in a straw Panama hat and a Sea Island tropical shirt, white chinos, and sandals approached us. His eyes were a doglike brown. His thin face conveyed cunning, distraction, a feral aptitude for double-dealing. He waved a handlettered sign: WAYNUTH SNITH.

"I am Manuel Duarte."

He smiled broadly, to show how perfectly intact his teeth were. Scars on his face told a different kind of story. "Welcome Inpector Snith and your friend to Venezuela! I am your driver and guide. Ask me for anything."

"Have you got a map of the city?"

Manuel Duarte shook his head.

"Ask me something else."

"You wouldn't happen to know if there have been any seizures of heroin lately, would you, Manuel?"

Duarte was leading us through a carpark to a drab blue Volvo sedan, battered on the passenger side.

Smith sat in front as Duarte drove. I could see our new companion had a superficially mild demeanor, and under that, the taut muscles and aggressive instincts of a born thug. Most police departments are full of thugs, and Manuel was, at least, not utterly repulsive to look at.

"I couldn't help you there." He swung into traffic, onto a cloverleaf that ascended onto another cloverleaf.

"No, actually, now I think, maybe they take some kilos mixed with a shipment of cocaine. Heroin is brown, or isn't it?"

"Sometimes," I interjected.

"And those confiscations, I take it," Smith uttered in a grand way, "would be in the police impound."

Caracas veered into view. Another scythe-shaped magnet of shit like all modern cities, and poorly situated to avoid going underwater in the next decade or so. *Ergo* boom town.

Landfills of artificial peninsulas extruded from the hub, ringed by artificial islands. These, it was said, were being grabbed up by the world's wealthiest who could not obtain private islands in Dubai.

"Things, they disappear from the impound right and left."

Duarte cocked an inquisitive eyebrow. What a creep, I thought. Doesn't waste any time on chitchat.

"Same the world over." Smith assumed a sad, worldly air, shaking his head. "Who were the villains, this time?"

"Fokking mutherfokking Catalina Brothers, down from their *favelas* to celebrate Chavulot or whatever they call it. Some Jewish thing. Fokking kike gangsters."

The traffic in Caracas had the ebb and flow of a decapped fire hydrant: it whizzed out in waves and dried up like a mirage. The buildings rose like razor blades from surging shanty villages where peasants beat laundry on rocks in marsh water.

"Were you the lead on the Catalina Brothers caper?"

Smith shamelessly sucked up to this admittedly quick-eyed but obvious cipher with a driver's license. Manuel Duarte wasn't likely to head up anything besides the precinct mail room. Too smart for his own good, and too stupid for anyone else's.

"No? I had just assumed, somehow."

Oh really, I thought, that's laying it on with a trowel. Smith paused. Collected thoughts. Dropped his voice just enough to convey his moral neutrality towards criminal enterprise.

"Hard to imagine someone with your skills has to drive visiting coppers all over creation." Smith confided this as if being able to drive had revealed Duarte as a man of multiple talents.

"See the News Tower? Largest structure in northern South America." Duarte seemed proud of a windowless cement monolith with a blinking red beacon on top of it.

"Tell me something, Manuel. *Mano a mano*. When things go missing from the impound, who gets it in the neck?"

Duarte's face curdled with ferocious feeling.

"That fatass sonbitch fokkhead, Luis Castella Rodriguez. Never at his post. Sits there on his fat ass in the strip bar across the street, Nola's Nook. Right through his shift. Waddles the fat ass over to the impound once an hour, sticks his nose in the door. Then back to Nola's. He has the stiff catzo for Carmen

Gheeha, star attraction at Nola's. Fat chance that fatass has. She can pick up razor blades with her twat, bending all the way backward. She juggles Ginsu knives with her ass cheeks. One time I saw her light her nipples on fire and squash the flames out on the patron's birthday cake. What would a woman like that want with a man like Luis Castella Rodriguez?"

From my perspective in the rear seat, the question sounded reasonable.

"He even tries to fuck my sister once. She's a lay nun who does good works among the poor who are everywhere. As you can see for yourself. I ask myself: how can such a piece of human *mierde* exist? Because his mother, she spread her legs for anybody. She is fucked one time by some fatass worthless drunk. Nine months later, presenting Luis Castella Rodriguez, Twisted Fuck of Venezuela. They should collect that sperm, if they knew where it came from, and use it as a biological weapon."

The News Tower could be seen from anywhere in the city, it appeared. It also seemed to see everything in the city, every movement on the human chessboard.

"This Rodriguez, he'd be in a bad spot if someone looted the impound while he was trying to romance Carmen Gheeha, I imagine?"

"Shit yes." Duarte chewed briefly at his moustache. "Especially if the looters took the dope *and* the automatic rifles confiscated from the Catalina Hacienda. Because it is well known, my friend, that Luis Castella Rodriguez has contacts with the NAOEC."

I had heard this acronym somewhere. In the *Financial Times*, possibly.

"North American Oil Extracting Contractors. They push and push for their drill bit leasing masters in Texas. And befoul Venezuela with their capitalist filth, ravenous for gain. They have no desire to help the working man or woman. They take one big crap all over the working man or woman. To them, proletariat is the name of a race horse."

Proletariat was, in fact, the name of a horse, moreover one that had won the Kentucky Derby for two consecutive years.

"Tell me something." Smith lit his ganja pipe. "In principle, are you opposed to putting a little elbow grease behind Rodriguez's *via con dios* from the department?"

Manuel Duarte didn't have to think about it. Smith had an instinct.

Part of our bond, as well as our emotional abrasion, was his neurotic need to astonish me with tricks he pulled out of his sleeve. The bonus-point miles on airline travel were likewise useful perks. But at times, Smith's maniacal deductions did nothing more than convince me that Fu Manchu was not the only person in the global equation with Multiple Personality Disorder.

"And you know," Duarte told him, breaking a long unthoughtful silence as the car windows drooled reflected neon signage, mostly in Chinese, some in Spanish, "if some of the missing items were to fall into the hands of our... neighboring brothers and sisters in strife..."

"Surely they need the weapons. Most of them, anyway."

They now had become conspirators.

"And some of the dope, Inpector Snith. Distasteful as the idea of it is to all our comrades. You can't break into an omelette without a few eggs."

Manuel steered the crushed-in, blue Volvo through a maze of back alleys, the streets shiny from oil and rain.

"All they want," he stated quietly, "is to bring the sweet fruit of democracy to their raped and butchered lands. Ruled by scum, their people lack only the weaponry and a modicum of drug money to drive the oligarchy back to the hell from which it came."

Quite a flourish for Duarte. Perhaps he wasn't what he appeared to be. But then, he'd probably memorized some political pamphlet.

Smith, naturally, was several mental steps ahead of Duarte's cognitive process, already mulling over the question of what four-wheel drive vehicle would enable us to reach the accursed plateau of the kanaimà.

"That whole wing of the building," Duarte told Smith, not at all fazed, giving us a gloss on the local architectural curiosities between unpleasant chortles, "is empty as a flushed toilet."

"Locked up like Fort Knox, I'll bet."

"Locked up tight as Rodriguez's mother's chastity belt is more like it," Duarte quipped. He began laughing so hard it took the wind out of him. Excessively amused at his own jape, the true sign of an imbecile.

I could embroider things and say that looting the police impound was fraught with peril, and describe every suspenseful detail, providing each creak of a forbidden door, but if it had been any simpler, I would've suspected a set-up.

The only fly in the ointment – and he did resemble a fly, somehow, something translucent in his face, like the transparency of fly's wings – was a uniformed policeman who appeared suddenly at the barred sign-in window of the lockup as we piled AK-47s, Kalashnikovs, and crates of other munitions for removal, as well as several bags of pure skag. This hapless cop nattered on about some blood sample evidence he needed for a court case the following a.m. Smith artfully worked his way out of the enclosure, pretended to consult the cop's requisition sheet, and, using a lug wrench, smashed the man's skull open. A minor glitch, all things considered.

"Eeesh," said Manuel, gingerly stepping over the lake of spreading blood from the cop's noggin. "I'll fetch a Jeep from our fleet." He looked down at the mess. "Is brother-in-law of the Chief."

"Oh dear." Smith fluttered. Yet he wore the triumphant look he always wore when he'd rendered a potential threat unpotential.

Duarte's throaty guffaw could have meant anything.

"I promise you, Waynuth Snith, nothing could delight our Head of Department more than an early expiration on this worthless peasant dog. It was a marriage of convenience, but the convenience turned out to be all this piece of shit's. The Chief has hated this prick like a bad case of crabs ever since he first laid eyes on him."

He paused before fetching the Jeep.

"And now, the Chief and the comely Marguerite can resume their – well, perhaps I should not say too much on this subject."

Duarte, evidently, knew Smith's destination, and felt less than jubilant about escorting him there. Yet now and again he dissembled his cowardly fear of the kanaimà with bravado.

We loaded the canvas compartment at the rear of a military Jeep well before Duarte's *bête noire*, Rodriguez, stuck his hourly nose into the compound.

We threaded, or rather lurched, down an alleged road through the rainforest with fifteen kilos of smack and an arsenal worthy of an Iowa klavern.

"You do understand," Duarte expatiated, "these kanaimà filth, they are not the Rotary Club. One kanaimà is another kanaimà's unbearable stink. There was only one real tribe of them long ago in the dream time, though they band together for ritual killings. That tribe wiped itself out like that." Snapped his fingers. Blew his nose into them afterwards and flung the snot out into the darkness. "Kanaimà become kanaimà for revenge. They don't do their disgusting ritual acts for a hobby. If I told you how disgusting, you would abandon this journey into the cursed valley. I take my own life into my hands. Only for the sake of my revolutionary brothers and sisters, not meaning yourselves."

Meaning, expect betrayal, if things fuck up.

Smith kept his left-hand pinkie fingernail long and sniff-ready, and was already sampling one of the kilo bags for purity.

"Oh, Petrie, if this doesn't set your anus atingle, nothing ever will. 99 and 1/100% pure as Ivory Snow."

Nothing relaxed Smith the way pure powder did. His eyes scanned the poorly visible span ahead as if it were a Disney animation.

I helped myself. Constipation is a small price to pay for such ecstasy.

"Manuel." His words came few and far between nods. "Tell Petrie." Smith gestured like a sloth, his arms attempting expressive gestures he forgot to complete. "About the kanaimà. The fermentation thing." High as a goat on an escarpment on Machu Picchu.

"You find something amusing about the fermentation? The most disgusting of all the kanaimà horrors?" Duarte hadn't dipped into the pleasure powder and his indignation sent Smith and me into peals of merriment. He swerved into the right shoulder of the primitive road to avoid hitting a possum and her offspring.

"No no, you misunderstand."

Smith couldn't stop laughing.

"Here we are… careening through jungle fever with one broken headlight… under a canopy of… richly evolved micro-ecosystems evolved over… millenia, if not more…"

"And soon it will all be bulldozed to graze beef cattle for McDonald's," Duarte said, indifferently.

"Better drive this heap more steady on, or we'll all make a farewell bonus meal."

Smith gazed around at the barely visible vegetation. There was nothing to see with that pure smack in his brainpan.

"Filthy world we're living in."

"*Filth* isn't the word. We're in a swirling toilet of our own shit," said Duarte with vehemence. I whooped with laughter.

Smith couldn't speak. His eyes had seen the glory. "Slaughtering each other, and then with these kanaimà, you have to wonder – what pleasure do they get to watch an enemy slowly wither away out of fear of the attack he knows is certain, but no idea what day, what month, what year? They let them know they are marked. With a beating, sometimes. Or some parrot feathers on their doorstep. Even just by whistling a certain way when the victim walks in the jungle. I shit on these kanaimà. I piss and puke and make shit on these kanaimà scum."

The rainforest. Headlamps banding trees. I knew Duarte was speaking the truth.

9

"We imagine a body without limbs when we imagine the ego," said the sibiline, disembodied-seeming menace in the voice emanating from the palpable, but close to evaporative emaciation, whose skin, a jaundice-yellow membrane adhering so tightly to a subdural array of things his interlocutor resisted imagining contained anything like human viscera – a single hit-or-miss assault with a can of spray paint could just as easily serve to restrain whatever lurked in the thing's innards from seepage, or prevent the stuff's sudden explosion out of the insidious doctor's unconvincingly humanoid body.

The prisoner now clung to a disappearing remnant of hope that he and his daughter would be released after their captor had no further use for them, rather than disposed of by protracted tinkering with their gene sequences by his successor, followed by their gang rape, either during or after their deliberately inept dismemberment by the same assortment of slant-eyed thugs.

Ken Jay no longer deflected such ethnophobic thoughts when they passed through his reptilian brain synapses. He no longer feared that the laboratory-generated monstrosities the little girl had only glimpsed as yet could inflict severe psychic mutilation. Even when it was a fear from (so far) just the sight of things compared to which a living hell sounded to him like a seafront condo in Maui.

90

There were still worse horrors hatching, he well understood, behind the terrifyingly calm figure wearing a diaphanous blue silk robe, embroidered with the ChoFatDong emblem of coiled snakes sinking fangs into a human embryo.

This eminence held a petrifying, steady gaze with his emerald-green eyes – demonic eyes which glowed in the dark, the squirming figure seated across the afromosia-inlaid desk felt certain.

The sinister, soft-spoken, murderously unblinking Mandarin's beard ran like a tapered shrink-wrapped ponytail from the cleft of his sallow, pointed chin. He had a glabrous forehead. The lugubriously studied movements of a junkie on the nod. The mind of three geniuses stuffed into a noggin dedicated to evil. Not pure evil, necessarily. Impure evil would do just fine.

"But the ego is nothing but paranoia and confusion. We throw up every imaginable defense mechanism against the unveiling of our nonexistence.

"Now," the imperious, long-nailed apparition hissed at the chubby East Indian geneticist in the white surgical smock, known as Ken Jay. "On this quiet *avenida*, with its villas set back from the thoroughfare, each walled, bearing a plaque of solid gold, engraved with a Teutonic last name... have walked some of the most prolific and inventive war criminals of the last century. I have outlived all these Aryan scum, thanks to my serum. All except the former man who calls herself Mildred Pretzelle."

"Of course you have, my Master." The pudgy gene splicer from Poona cringed. "I have never personally seen this Mildred Pretzelle with my own eyes."

"She, or he, as you prefer, seldom ventures out. Something – " the ancient figure chortled as if savoring a fond memory " – went terribly wrong with his or her sex reassignment surgery. It seems Mildred Pretzelle, so-called, was planning a surreptitious visit home to Oberhausen. Alas, the best laid plans of mice and Pretzelles..."

Ken Jay shuddered, more to satisfy the Master's wish to scare him out of his wits than out of any frightful image of what might have run awry during such a surgical procedure.

"When will the cultures be ready?" snapped the Master.

"I should think any time now."

"Any time now is not an answer," replied Dr. Fu Manchu, for the spectral figure was none other than the world's foremost impresario of malignant pranks and unnatural fatalities.

"Next Monday?"

"Unless you wish to have Lilah fed to the burrowing centipedes," Fu casually remarked, buffing a stupendously long fingernail with an emery board, "I'd get the lead out of your keester and take that ridiculous smock off unless you have a lobotomy to perform this afternoon, and make it Sunday for the cultures."

"Please, all-seeing, all-knowing, all-singing, all-dancing Master of the Universe, I beg of you. Not the burrowing centipedes, even if I should fail."

Ken Jay dropped to the Amritsar carpet in a persiflage of grovelling admiration for the maniacal savant who controlled him and used his expertise for the manufacture of hideous insects, loathsome viruses…

"Feed ME to the centipedes, if you must, I beg you, but spare my daughter the indignity and agony of insect death!"

Fu rose and paced in his gliding manner, his face a mask of inscrutable malevolence.

"I am not without a sense of mercy," he finally crooned. "Should you fail, considering what is at stake, I shall allow you the experience of the exquisite torture of the burrowing centipedes, despite the deficient nourishment you would provide with your excessive body fat. Perhaps Lilah, instead, will receive the Zaybar Kiss. Do not ask me what it is, for I do not know. But I can summon it with a snap of my fingers. And don't imagine I cannot snap my fingers, because of my long nails. You'd be very much mistaken. It's an acquired skill. More trouble than it's worth, really, but far from impossible."

The demoralized Ken Jay shrugged as if it were all the same to him, aware that any further special pleading would fall on delightedly indifferent ears. Fu cared nothing for anything, except his pet marmoset, Cutie. This creature now scrambled up Fu's chair as the Master resumed his office posture, and nestled under his chin.

"There you go, my precious sweetie-sweet, daddy's little love-bucket, give Fu a kiss, give silly Fu some Cutie kisses…"

Cutie, Ken Jay had to concede, really was cute, all hairy and fluffy and batlike, and he reminded himself that a pet doesn't get to pick its owner. If Cutie seemed fanatically attached to the aspiring architect of Mandarin world supremacy, it was obviously because Fu Manchu fed him. For an animal to know where its next meal is coming from can only ever be a stroke of great luck.

Fu Manchu was too much a chip off the Nosferatu block to let things alone, and had trained his adorable mammal companion to bare its razory fangs and fling itself violently back and forth in its cage, when Cutie was in his cage, if any other human being offered Cutie a snack. Fu's perversity knew no boundaries Ken Jay could think of, though Ken Jay was keenly aware of his own lack of imagination.

The unspeakable imprisonment of Lilah, Ken Jay's daughter and favorite concubine, could only spell trouble in Chinese or English – the burrowing centipedes, the Zaybar Kiss, none of these diabolisms worried the geneticist nearly as much as the possibility that Fu Manchu, who, thanks to his longevity serum, could not have been a day younger than 140, still had the eager libido of a 90-year-old. He'd already turned Lilah into a mesmerized agent of his bidding, but what if this wizened, green-eyed master of darkness fixed his slobbering amorous attention on the still-virginal Lilah?

Ken Jay again shuddered, involuntarily this time, at the idea of having Fu Manchu as a son-in-law. Not only would Lilah be sapped of her natural exuberance, as to some degree she already had, but Ken Jay would have to sit through interminable Chinese meals with endless courses, while Fu Manchu expounded his so-called philosophy and denounced the decadent civilization of the West. And gloated. Fu's gloating truly tested one's intestinal fortitude. One area that hadn't fared well throughout the insane doctor's repeated administrations of his serum was his buccal orifice and the teeth contained therein. Way more plaque than could possibly be healthy for him.

10

At Land's End, events now moved at an unfamiliar clip.

For anything at all to occur at Land's End was itself a bird of bad omen, a sign of blight and ruination. I mean worse than usual.

I escaped Petrie's house before it became an asylum, locking it against further incursions by blabbering hysterics, and ventured across the town.

Marco's carriage house, off Blowbladder Street. Tucked behind tall weedy grass and a bamboo screen. The West African appears in a casual pair of Gap khakis, a rust-colored turtleneck sweater, barefoot. He offers tea.

In the cottage, a narcotic calm, a cry of wheeling sea birds overhead.

Alfred Schnittke's cello compositions, played by whom I do not know. Soon this wafting background segues into Couperin: "Laudate pueri Dominum," sung by a virtuoso I can't identify, whose cadences are so flawless that all that I hate and love about liturgical motets are gathered within them. Something... fatalistic in perfection, as if having nothing to do with life, but with a spiritual plane I have no belief in whatever.

"No doubt there's been a lot of talk."

Marco's ethereality, standing beside his own full-length portrait at right angle to a convex mirror in the place one expects to find coatracks and such, stirs his tea. My cup chatters in my fingers like wind-up toy teeth.

"There's always a lot of talk. Especially at Petrie's."

Marco's pensive eyebrow.

"Any word from Petrie?"

The coach house's seductive aroma, as if horses quartered in it long ago left the afterscent of their sweaty exertions.

I provide the negative answer Marco expects.

"Gossip galore at the Scroop from Field Marshall Rahmschnitzel, as usual. Funny atmosphere. Something's thrown things into a fester over there. The flautist's disappeared. Talk is she may've met the same fate as Fanny Bacon, though god knows why."

Marco nods.

"Nothing worse than what that swine Sauerbrotten deserves."

Between his shapely brown fingers a thin black cigarette.

A fireplace sends varicolored flames from a Duraflame log.

Works of art framed on the oyster-grey walls. A ghostly portrait by Witkiewicz of Jadwiga Janczewska, from 1914. A Seurat pencil drawing in braided lines, of the part of an old woman's hair, from overhead, as she embroiders. A monkey poised on all fours. A reclining female nude in the Modigliani manner.

Marco separating tangled filaments of facts invisible to anyone else. The ash of his long cigarette flaking on the floor.

His face: I know something you don't.

"Coming over…" I broke the silence, or bent it, anyway. "I saw some nocturnals wandering. Looking blinded by sunlight. Unnerving."

"It's starting."

More distressing quiet.

"Apothecary's had a run on paregoric."

"It isn't just withdrawal."

The coach house was swank for its surroundings. Deceptively Olde England on the outside, peeling shutters, brass doorknock, geraniums in windowboxes.

"This Fanny affair…"

Time slowed.

"I feel in my bone it's just the beginning."

I put away the tea things.

"Tell you what. We'll walk round to Khartovski's. There's some developments."

Night mist and a three-quarter moon. Wood smells on a breeze.

Khartovski inhabited the bottom floor of a three-family house halfway up a steep hill. Pale hedges chalky white from years of indifferent pruning. Stunted fruit trees. The would-be Ettrick Shepherd possessed an out-of-key upright in one of the rooms. Once he'd played Glinka or Schumann for company but that habit died with the town's only piano tuner.

One of his many economies was the parsimonious use of electric light. Khartovski's duck-egg head, braided moustaches, and piercing black eyes appeared in an almost unreadable darkness, dispelled by a candle in a pewter holder.

The inner room flickered with more candlelight. An oak table took up most of the room. A figure sat there, half-obscured by the shifting shadows. She had an array of little objects on the table she was busy winding up.

"Oh." Khartovski looked at Marco uncomfortably.

Marco twisted his lips into withering superiority.

"Don't panic. We haven't come for that."

He noticed the girl at the far end of the table. The draft subsided, exposing her face and arms, the hands of the vexed-looking flautist from Zryd's orchestra.

"*You* couldn't cause me to panic."

"Ah." Marco's radar was up. "You've been having second thoughts?"

Khartovski withheld a response. He'd had more than a few second thoughts, evidently. My thought was how well Marco hid the qualities that enabled him to score a fortune in small arms deals.

The flautist looked at us without interest. She was winding up mechanical toys, setting them loose on the tabletop: a miniature Godzilla, a set of chattering teeth, a penis mounted on mechanical legs. She watched their progress like a horse race.

She stared at us after a minute or so. Lowered her eyes, smiled contemptuously.

"Vanessa Savage." She introduced herself with harsh emphasis on the family name.

"Not to worry," Khartovski told her. "He's an old friend."

The noisy Japanese toys reached the exhaustion of their wire springs. Godzilla pitched over on its side.

"Old friends are the ones you should worry about," she said. "You planning to tell them now?"

"Sure. No time like the present."

"No time *but* the present," she corrected. "I'll tell them. It will give me pleasure."

She looked defiant, challenging in a seductive way. She was a perfect gamine with raccoon eyes. Tougher, though. Quick, and, as I soon realized, full of exasperation at the stupidity of the world around her. As if daring life to kill her, knowing it wouldn't – not any time soon. A fearlessness at odds with her delicate face and lithe body, or maybe it wasn't.

11

Roswitha Klebb has switched sides in the war between Scotland
Yard and the ChoFatDong so many times she forgets now and
then which side she works for. She's a valuable asset for both. If
she weren't, Roswitha Klebb and her club foot would've turned
up years ago as skeletal remains in a Siberian peat bog.

Roswitha has teamed herself once more with Dr. Fu Manchu
and the ChoFatDong, enabling her to turn a tidy profit on
counterfeit CDs, smuggled nuclear isotopes, and fake Chanel
dresses in the very fulcrum of world crime, Ciudad del Este, at
the eastern border of Paraguay.

Ciudad del Este is a violence-riddled spit of red-dirt
Paraguayan wasteland, reclaimed in the last century for use as a
mecca for money laundering and the rapid translation of stolen
and counterfeit everything into squeaky clean bank deposits
in the Caymans. Festooned with storefront mosques, crude
billboards, and precariously tossed-up highrise buildings. This
suits Roswitha as well as anything else.

She is a profoundly unhappy individual of 50, ever-spreading
waistline, criminal proficiency unmatched by all but the most
exalted elites of freebootery and intricately planned homicides,
currently the housebound dispatcher for two different gangs of
carjackers, clubfoot to boot. And, within her elephantine bosom,
a heart beating in syncopation with unassuagable sadness of

loss, soured into bottomless bitterness and rue. And the desire for revenge, against all kinds of people.

For, once upon a time, while employed by the East German STASI, Roswitha had experienced a summer love, the summer love celebrated in song, the summer love lamented when the leaves of autumn flutter down to form a burnished K-Mart Martha Stewart throw carpet upon fallow field and frost-shrivelled glen.

The man in question was, and to this day is, a dangerously elegant, multilingual, sexually inexhaustible, and generally suspicious fountain of adventure *vis-à-vis* impossible-to-unravel methods of assassination, Johann Schmitz-Fitzpatrick, whose protean, wriggling seed scored a direct hit on one of Roswitha's eggs on the first (and last) shot out of his tunnel of love, producing, without benefit of clergy, nine months following, a plump and adorable little princess whom Roswitha named Beatrix, in homage of the Queen of the Netherlands, maven of the Bilderbergers, many of whose loyal subjects had vanished into pits of quicklime over the years under Roswitha's expert supervision.

Alas, Johann Schmitz-Fitzpatrick had not been put on earth to concern himself with any post-coital fructifications caused by his briskly peripatetic distribution of love custard throughout the female ranks of STASI agents and an array of neurotic nightclub songstresses. He regarded his thick, creamy globs of unusually propulsive "love juice" (he believed this was the correct expression in English) an enviable gift for any woman to receive. Sometimes, after his initial discharge, he would entertain his more droll-minded playmates by masturbating his gigantic member (as he imagined it, at least) until his volcanic spunk soared out of his glans like a guided missile, unerringly splattering against the ceiling, to the vast amusement of all who witnessed these feats of ejaculative marksmanship.

What an infatuated, crippled freak like Roswitha Klebb

did with the yeast-like growth developing from his frantic, last-minute scouring of female STASI personnel files in search of a phone number for an urgently needed dicksplash receptacle was Roswitha Klebb's problem. Johann had no intention of legitimizing, or even acknowledging, the existence of the winsome precocious Beatrix, the mere announcement of her incipience abruptly severing all connection between the powerful Schmitz-Fitzpatrick to the comparatively low-on-the-organization-totem-pole Klebb.

As they worked in different departments of STASI headquarters, it was simple enough for Johann to avoid any glimpse of his clubfooted one-off paramour, and a no-brainer to him to swiftly have her reassigned to another municipality.

Roswitha had, uncharacteristically, wept, pouted, and sunk into depressions for months after Johann's desertion, but this grief was as nothing to the heartbreak that smote her quite suddenly one evening when little Beatrix Klebb ran a soaring fever and had to be sped by ambulance to the Malenkov Pediatric Hospital in Leipzig, where Roswitha had been transferred to a STASI camp notorious for capricious torture of interrogation subjects, murder by lethal injections of pure heroin, and the most vicious women's volleyball team in the GDR.

That night, the purpuric fever little Beatrix had contracted proved resistant to antibiotics and, more alarming still, her toes and fingers began a process of self-amputation associated with this invariably fatal pediatric malady, indigenous to Brazil and, until then, unheard of in the GDR, or indeed anywhere in Europe. Vascular collapse followed within a few hours, and by daybreak the precocious Beatrix had floated, not without physical misery, back to the eternal flux from which she had but recently emerged.

The death of her child has changed Roswitha Klebb, from an enthusiastic sadist and assertive martyr to her deformed extremity, to a torpid, overweight, half-hearted specialist in artificially induced coronary trauma and the introduction of genetically amplified bacteria and other microorganisms into the bloodstreams of various agents, not all of them working for any sovereign government, determined to expunge Dr. Fu Manchu from the global conquest equation and seize control of the ChoFatDong.

Her mind, such as it is, has honed its primary object on subtle if sedentary plans designed to wreak as much havoc as she can manage. Her seventh-floor domain consists of seven rooms, three of which are piled to the ceiling with crates of contraband electronics merchandise, cigarette cartons looted from a retail smoke shack in North Carolina, and crates of heroin. Her living room, kitchen, and bedroom look very like the impersonally decorated flat she owns in Munich, while the remaining spaces serve as either storage areas or absolutely empty chambers of stagnant air.

At five p.m., Roswitha, recumbent on a modular sofa that tends to separate into its individual modules under her weight, watches footage of a recent terror bombing in a Polynesian resort hotel, with the sound off. The carnage flashing on screen fills her with warmth. *More human filth out of the way*, is Roswitha's thought.

She employs a speaker phone to endure one of Fu Manchu's exhaustingly verbose monologues, listening to every fourth or fifth word, awaiting instructions she knows from tediously long experience will not be forthcoming until Fu concludes his opium-dilated musings. The crackly, strangely compelling voice has much to tell her, much that he could easily tell his marmoset, or a stack of Pfaltzgraff dinnerware.

Roswith has never devised an effective method for getting Fu off the telephone. Even when glazed over entirely, some tireless receptors in her sensorium register every word he says. She considers without delight that he does, in fact, possess hypnotic powers that interfere with her concentration.

"…if we keep that klepto shitbird on at World Code, now that he's done his early parole thing courtesy of guess whose lawyer, who take my word for it doesn't do charity cases or pro bono, I want him on a short leash. We've had altogether too much data loss. How they managed to memory dump so much of it, when it was stored on seven different mainframes, is either a mystery for the ages, or some type of elaborately planned industrial sabotage, and I am inclined towards the latter explanation…

"Ah, Fräulein Klebb, the headaches that come with empire building would put Tiger Balm out of inventory. They make me yearn for a simpler life. A little island somewhere, with pristine beaches, uneventful days, and nights of perfect weather…"

Roswitha can't resist planting her sharp-edged oar into the puddle of this purported fantasy of his.

"You *have* a little island somewhere. You have nine little islands, last time I counted, including one ten miles out from Cartagena. If you hopped a flight right now and changed in Bogota for the coastal shuttle, you could be having mai tais on the veranda in six hours."

Fu, as is his wont, does not hear anything she says.

"But no, nothing doing, no palmy paradises and sedative sunsets for yours truly, when you're Fu Manchu, Klebb, everything that manages to crawl from the woodwork shows up with a handful of gimme and a mouthful of much oblige. I'm up to my pigtail in complications, day in, day out. My nemesis is rooting around as we speak up in kanaimà country, with that junkie doctor of his."

Pot calling the kettle black, Roswitha thinks, rolling her exophthalmic eyes, one of her many unalluring features. She pictures Fu cooking up a nice heirloom spoonful of H while droning on at her. He *would* wriggle the thought of dope into her head, thoughtless as always, everything always has to be all about Fu, his problems, his drugs, his life-extending elixir, his army of freeze-dried seven-year-olds or whatever they are, his latest genetically mutated bugs, his torment over choosing the right shade of fingernail polish.

Never her, never Roswitha Klebb, hell no, what's a little irritant like a club foot, an untameable weight problem, a recently deceased child, and moving depleted fuel rods across the Brazilian border in a lead-lined shoulder bag that weighs about a thousand pounds, stumping across the Friendship Bridge on her clomping foot in its square boot, arousing endless, stifled mirth among the border guards. Roswitha roots around for her remote and switches the image on the wall-sized plasma screen to her favorite Brazilian telenova.

While Fu yaks away, Roswitha reads the actors' lips, but she knows roughly what is transpiring. Oduvaldo's office affair with Bruna, despite the slow, methodical manner in which the unspeakably handsome young executive has introduced progressively more distance between them, encouraging Bruna to date other men, has on Bruna's part developed into an entirely phoney, consuming passion that will almost certainly, somehow, result in Oduvaldo's wife, Sibelia, learning of his infidelity. Not only that, Bruna claims she has a cake in the oven, though Oduvaldo, who has no concrete reason to disbelieve it, picked up something in Bruna's voice when she first made this announcement sound distinctly smug and unmaternal.

Sluts like Bruna always know who the father is, Oduvaldo reflects bitterly, Roswitha imagines, sluts like Bruna having never experienced True Love. In every case, whichever guy she's been banging who's got the biggest bank account is definitely Dad. And Bruna means to get her hands on every penny of his – unless the shadow of a plan that began forming in Oduvaldo's mind several episodes ago might somehow advance to the instrumentation stage – by means of the cardboard bundle of joy she's invented. Bruna couldn't care less if her unscrupulous machinations cause poor Sibelia an early grave and Oduvaldo's own mind to go spinning off its spool. All the better for that deranged Bolivian strumpet, if he were stupid enough to marry her, which he isn't. She'd leave him to rot in some nuthouse while jetting all over the continent on what she probably imagines will be an eternal shopping spree.

Poor dumb Bruna. If she only knew the kind of financial cul-de-sac Oduvaldo and Sibelia have been trapped in for the past two years, entirely dependent on familial largesse that can be snipped short at any moment, she might discover that the real progenitor of this make-believe blob of tissue inside her is none other than Lionel, the retarded twenty-two-year-old, mongoloid son of the company's owner, "Tippy" Tapir.

Oduvaldo's musings are not purely cynical, wishful thinking. He knows, thanks to a janitor's tip-off, that Bruna cornered the drooling Lionel in the unisex handicapped bathroom on the fifth floor roughly seven weeks ago and initiated him into a somewhat spastic, predictably inept approximation of sexual intercourse, an act which Lionel did not entirely grasp the purpose of, and which very nearly didn't come off, so to speak, despite Bruna's fierce, ruthless tenacity. Dumping Oduvaldo for the retard would by no means preclude Bruna spilling to Oduvaldo's wife, "through the grapevine," because Bruna's greatest joy is making harmless, well-meaning people suffer, repaying kindness with treachery, and generosity with base ingratitude that often involves potentially career-wrecking slanders.

Of course Oduvaldo knows he isn't blameless in the matter, and should have had a keener radar for Bruna's peasant notions of social advancement. Indeed, Bruna has recently threatened to pay a surprise visit to their home unless Oduvaldo agrees to divorce Sibelia. Oduvaldo has no intention of doing any such thing: Bruna's faked, devouring love has become a source of escalating terror, especially since she hardly makes their intense lunchtime jiggy-jiggy at the nearby Curitiba Mojito Hotel a secret at work any more, and one of his fiercely competitive colleagues will inevitably spill to a spouse, who will then be all too avid to drop witlessly obvious hints to Sibelia.

Furthermore, Bruna barely scraped through secretarial school, lives in a sordid furnished room uncomfortably close to a hillside *favela* full of murderous drug gangs and professional killers, and her people are even lower than peasants, a tribe of petty thieves and blackmailing barn-burners who oozed their way into Brazil by slipping across the Bolivian frontier into Mato Grosso, disguised as Carmelite nuns on a pilgrimage to the Basilica of Aparecida, each with two kilos of pure cocaine strapped under their habits. A whole family of cons. Oh yes, Oduvaldo has had this bimbo's number for a considerable time. Her scummy clan was running a big store scene in Bahia before slouching towards São Paolo.

Why has he immured himself in this mess? He could simply have her shot in the street; Oduvaldo's brother, Javier, owns a Kalashnikov and a vintage WWII Luger and a bunch of other suitable weapons, and he knows Javier would let him put it on the tab. But why, why has he gotten in so deep with such a shallow, scungy nothing? She has a fabulous body, magnificent tits, an ass that would raise a zombie from the tomb, but virtually nothing between her ears besides her forehead and a lot of criminal impulses, no social advantages to offer, a growing tendency to whine and pout and drizzle lachrymose sentiments when she feels neglected – virtually all the time, really. He has tried to talk her into an abortion but nix on stix, that tiny tumor in her uterus is, so to speak, Bruna's little ace in the hole. Except Oduvaldo has never believed for an instant there's really anything in there besides the usual contents of her gooey snatch. She's keeping up the flimsy fiction, all the same. She hasn't crossed the threshold of a church since the age of twelve, but claims her Roman Catholic faith precludes the very thought of terminating the future three-card-monte entrepreneur burgeoning inside her, as Oduvaldo thinks of it, gestating like mold on a six-week-old lemon.

He's argued that a baby will wreck Bruna's life, that even if he left Sibelia the three ruddy little youngsters she's incubated during their marriage will drain away his income in child support payments, giving birth will stretch Bruna's pussy out of all recognition, that she will no longer find herself free to dash out to the movies or a disco bar on a moment's notice with her girlfriends, and so forth. Bruna has a ready answer to every complication Oduvaldo raises. Where there is love, Bruna's wordless lips intone, all obstacles vanish, like a turd in a septic tank!

"Are you listening to me, Klebb?"

"I'm always listening to you, oh Master of the Universe…"

"Very funny. Too bad you're busy flopping around on your keester, if you could see the startling progress we've made with the Cold Children! And that's only the start of something big, Klebb. Big and cold as Antarctica before we melted it down, and deadly as the neurotoxins of a gaboon viper." Fu Manchu's thrilled-sounding voice breaks off, as if the Mandarin of Morbidity has been radically distracted from what promised until then to develop into a rousing exhortation. "You don't think that little bitch is going to trap him into walking out on Sibelia and the kids, do you?" It just bursts out of him uncontrollably.

I knew it, Roswitha chortles to herself.

"Well, Fu, look what she did last episode. First she sent the dry cleaning receipt for that Prada outfit the big O was fool enough to buy her, accidentally-on-purpose, to Oduvaldo's father-in-law. Then she used the power of the pussy to wheedle Quando the gardener into tampering with the brake lining on Sibelia's Lexus. If she hadn't lent the car to her sister, rest her soul, it would've been Sibelia's head that landed in the cab of that sixteen-wheeler. Let's face it, Bruna will stop at nothing."

"Damn it," Fu Machu wheezes in his opiate-saturated voice. "Look what you made me do. I got all involved in this and just spilled a whole beaker of modified centipedes all over the

Missoni sweaters I was planning to give Reynaldo. I mean if he gets back alive any time soon."

"*I* made you – my god, Fu, you really *are* paranoid! If you didn't insist on handling all these specimens with those finger-nails of yours, that's how Madame Curie bought the farm you know – "

"Ugly little pisspoor excuses for deadly insects," mutters Fu. "You know, we had them bite one of the Africans about seven times and all that happened was, the guy said, 'Ouch, that stings!' And frankly, I think he only said that to make me feel more omnipotent. You know, Klebb, I've been thinking… what if Ken Jay did some type of genetic splice of these Chilopoda arthropods with a whole different phylum? Something that's been extinct for a while, like those greenish, what do you call them, the trilobites or whatever they are my minions uncovered during the Tibetan Excavations, the ones with the vestigial wings and the double dorsal spines?"

Now Roswitha has stopped listening to her current master.

"Look, see? Oduvaldo *never* gave Bruna that bracelet. Unbelievable. Wearing it right to the office and waving it in everybody's face. That cunt bribed the maid to pilfer it and make sure Sibelia noticed it was missing. Oh, god, that rotten tart is trying to drive poor Sibby to suicide or insanity. And right after killing her sister. It's all coming out in the wash, this time. And he's such a coward. Why doesn't he just tell her himself, tell her how sorry he is, put a bit of effort into making it up to her… Unless – "

"Unless Sibelia's so-called friend Claudia comes clean about the switcheroo with the gynecologist. That's a big *unless*, Roswitha, don't lose track of all the skeletons in Claudia's closet Bruna wormed out of her the night they got drunk at the bowling alley."

"Yes, but that was two whole seasons ago, when the other actress played Claudia. Remember the Barbara Steele type they had for a while? I think the writers just dropped that whole subplot, it really wasn't going anywhere. I think Claudia's a schizo, I honestly do. She just *thinks* she has a chequered past she has to hide from everybody. All you have to do is look at her, you can see nothing's ever happened to Claudia in her life."

Roswitha stumps over to the gold-threaded rayon curtains along the vast window that provides a much too generous view of Ciudad del Este's sordid downtown district, tugs at the looped cord, and slowly allows the panorama of this lawless frontier town that might have been transplanted whole from the American Wild West to fill her field of vision.

"Feh," she says, really feeling something vile in the pit of her stomach. "Talk about a dump worth vaporizing." She has suddenly gleaned, in a nebulous way, the parallels between her own miserable history and the current plot of "Más feo que el Pecado."

"Are those Marlboros moving at all?"

And a micromanager from hell, like Fidel Castro, reflects Roswitha. She pictures a world ruled by Fu Manchu: he'd even design the postage stamps. Maybe I should take that offer from the Muslim Brotherhood but I'm not wearing that fucking veil. Mother always said my mouth was my best feature.

"We can't even unload them on the day tourists. They refuse to believe they're *originale*. They've got tax stamps on them and everything, what more do they want? Bonus coupons? Two for one? The fake Cartier watches are selling, though."

He's already seen the inventory, she thinks. He's trying to find out if I'm skimming. Like Anjelica Huston told that guy in *The Grifters*, either somebody's skimming a little or they're skimming a lot. As far as the watches are concerned, she's skimming plenty.

"I bet we did better with the Rolexes, though."

It's right there on the fax, she thinks. Maybe he can't make it out, too cheap to buy a new fax machine or go electronic with it. Too busy playing with bugs.

"Guess again."

Fu Manchu's voice once more drops to that whispery, theatrical ominousness he so enjoys putting on.

"And Klebb, what about…"

Oh spit it out, she thinks, we're on a secure line.

"What about what."

Like she didn't know. The biggest deal since they came down here. Total scam, which Roswitha loves the idea of.

"What about the fuel rods."

Some of Fu's people easily got security clearance jobs with ConEdison at the Indian Point Power Plant on the Hudson River. Spent fuel rods, nothing easier. Especially *really* spent ones. There is, she reflected, plenty of con in ConEdison anyway, but we've really upped the ante.

"Well, they still want the fuel rods, *avec* isotopes, they'll fucking cough up the scratch, or go back to parking fertilizer trucks in front of the wrong embassies."

Now, she expects, there will come a blistering tirade about cheapass Muslims, and she isn't far off the mark.

"But they said last week! Last Thursday!"

Roswitha, however, has dealt with enough megalomaniacs in one useless lifetime to cut this one off at the pass. I'd be good as a receptionist, she thinks. For World Code, maybe.

"They said, they said. *Will you listen to yourself?* I know you never listen to me, but if you would just once – oh, never mind. They *say* a lot of things, then you get the poor mouth. You know as well as I do. These terrorists are the cheapest bunch of lazy-ass fanatics I've ever had to deal with, and I'm including all those bastards in the STASI. 'Oooh, pleeease, can't we put the isotopes on the tab? Maybe some cesium-137 as a little sweetener?' What tab? I mean jesus b. christ, you'd think reactor fuel and bomb components grew on palm trees. It's that putrid-smelling supposedly sightless Sheik Abdullah Dabbu who runs that… Sizzler Mosque down there next to Pizza Hut.

Whips up the perfectly seasoned Steak and Malibu Chicken by feel – probably avian flu ostrich slices, everything tastes just like chicken to this bunch. Human flesh, grilled mynah bird – old blind Abbie Dabbu egging them on, mission's sacred, so something for nothing is his motto."

She hates the so-called blind sheik, or holy whatsis; for one thing he's not blind, it's a big act, like that Mafioso wandering around Little Italy a few years back in his bathrobe. People will fall for anything. That's why people who need people, Roswitha reminds herself, are the stupidest people in the world.

"I can see the little shits right from here, all stuffing their stringy beards with pepperoni. That's the fourth pizza they've scarfed down today. They sit there until two minutes before prayer time, then pop next door to the Sizzler. The Sizzler doesn't even face Mecca, Fu, these guys don't even respect their own jihad, just their fucking stomachs. It's no wonder they all look like melted cheese, it's the only thing they ever eat. You could serve them spicy crust molded *pork* and they'd think it was KFC in a bucket."

If anything gets her dander up more than having her telenova interrupted, it's the sight of all those religious fanatics, eating pizza. Of course, the beauty part is, she can see them from her windows, but they don't see her. She's managed to get several of their cars jacked by keeping a keen eye on that block. A BMW, a Buick Skylark, quite a few vintage numbers like you find in Havana.

"Roswitha, calm down. And don't be so harsh on our Muslim brothers. I know they're not such glowing examples of humanity."

"They will be, once they get those isotopes. They want the graphite lead casings, they can bloody well pay for the graphite lead casings. It's not like it's gonna break their little hawallah scam at that bogus Western Union."

Scratch the job offer from the Muslim Brotherhood. She

figures she could skim a fabulous sum running their hallawalah for a few weeks and then scram, get some surgical work done, but then what? Her clubfoot gives her away every time, unless she pretends the other one's deformed too: then she walks like a footbound Han dynasty fatty femme fatale.

"Yes, but they're trying to overthrow the capitalist system, same as we are."

There's another mistaken belief on Fu's part, she telepaths to the ignoramus Bruna on the screen, who, repugnant though she is, knows the score about the capitalist system, to a degree. Nothing can overthrow capitalism. It has to devour itself. That's the nature of it.

"Well," says Roswitha, her voice dripping with sarcasm, "that will be quite a trick if they spend all day eating the capitalist system's franchise pizza, then maybe a little chicken-fried steak with fries and some A-1 on the side, or a bucket of home-style wings, a couple sides of molasses-baked beans, some *onion rings* to remind them of all the pussy they're not getting, or each other's O rings they *are* getting in that hovel they live in… after prostrating themselves in front of the service counter long enough to thank Allah for inventing pole dancing and Blimpie's. They're praying to the goddam *cash register*, that Quaaba or whatever you call that stupid meteorite is in the completely opposite direction. Some of them even use *air mattresses* instead of a thin roll of cloth. And I'd hate to smell those socks they've got shoved in each other's faces."

Oduvaldo's father-in-law's face distorts in a rubber mask of distaste, seeing Bruna in his doorway. What on earth can this pig want with me, he must be thinking. And how dare she come here, of all places.

"What can you expect? They're a breakaway sect, number one, it's a whole generation of technocratic ignoramuses. They know how to blow themselves up with C4 – "

"Oh, like any of those losers really has the balls – " And

if they did, thinks Roswitha, what a bright world it would be. Brighter, anyway.

" – but they don't even know what year the Crusades started. They don't even know where *Canada* is, there's a survey right in the *Guardian* this morning – but we were kids once, Roswitha. They've got their own little ways, just like we did."

Roswitha does nothing to disguise her yawn. She's just taken four two-milligram Klonopin with some scotch, and it's kicking in.

"You're right, Fu. When were you ever, ever wrong. But let me say one thing, Oh Master of the Universe, when I was a little kid, you were over a hundred years old, so if you don't mind… I mean don't make me feel geriatric on top of ugly and fat and clubfooted, all I need is one more defect and I'm going out that fucking window. I mean if I can get the goddam thing open. I'll probably land on one of those assholes just as he's stuffing the last slice of pizza with *cheese baked right into the crust* down his gob. If you don't mind, I'd like to get off the phone and turn the volume up on this. I don't think she was saying what we thought she said."

"By all means, Fräulein Klebb. I, too, have… a little business to take care of."

"I bet he does end up divorcing her."

"I'm afraid you're probably right. He's spineless."

"If he's stupid enough to marry Bruna, she's in for a rude awakening. See, what she doesn't know," Roswitha adds with a malicious smile no one else can see, "is that *Sibelia's* family's the one with the money. And if they kill her, there's the revert in the trust fund. Oduvaldo's father is nothing but a *postal carrier*."

PART TWO
La Tormenta

12

Petrie here.

Like a sleep-starved hallucination, the Pisco Holiday Inn rose from barren flatness after miles and miles of scattered hovels, emaciated cows, scabs of dense vegetation between parched fields of witch grass and quadrants of fossilized mud. An occasional human-something flickered in doorless openings of thatch-roofed huts, or sluggardly limped behind snuffling, swaybacked black pigs; here and there, in the suffocating humidity of the paradoxically arid Yawong Valley, expressionless naked children squatted in dirt outside jerry-built shelters.

Yet there it stood, or sagged, a generic American-built motel in the standard two-tiered style, its units ranged around a cracked, empty swimming pool, its neon signage fissured and defunct office windows smashed, what had once been a coffee shop stripped of banquettes, steam tables, dishware; I wondered how, and when, this absurdity had ever attracted guests. Then recalled the lightning-short period of oil speculation when vast stretches of the much-publicized Yawong Valley were featured in newspaper photographs. Now pock-marked with "dry holes" that lent a lunar eeriness to that granite-inflected landscape, we had, I considered, arrived at the nadir of nothingness.

Once, these corridors had resounded with sparkling laughter and carefree voices, the pool a giddy froth of oil engineers

and teenage prostitutes from Georgetown, and the festive
kidney-shaped sign, powered by the Inn's expensive generator
– a hunk of rusted rubbish today, behind the main building,
near a crumbling tennis court and a crude, stinking privy – had
sent its pink and blue giggle of winking hospitality the length
and breadth of that disorienting wilderness of superstition,
annihilating poverty, and madness. A time of bright hope had
evaporated long ago, when the valley proved bare of any fossil
fuel deposits, and rich, in several substratum, in toxic gases
that, once tapped, sent geysers of lethal chemicals into the
atmosphere.

The various chambers and suites of the Pisco Holiday Inn
wore a dense wrinkle of decay, as if behind each door might be
revealed some long-dormant, recrudescent horror, or at best a
family of inbred squatters feeding on small lizards and boiled
scorpions.

"What a dump," I could not refrain from saying.

"Consider the source," Manuel Duarte retorted under his
breath.

Since our initial encounter with Duarte, he had segued
through several personality types, to my way of viewing things,
at least. At bottom, he was just another mercenary slob, I
thought.

The truth is, you never know who you're really dealing with
until you really know who you're dealing with, and, of course,
quite often you are dealing with several people at the same time
in the form of a single individual. I had more or less concluded
that this could be the case with Manuel Duarte. A short con
artiste. None of the individuals who were him were particularly
appetizing.

The Jeep tore into the long-disintegrated parking lot, hitting
fissures and potholes, Duarte's face a grimace of distaste, as
if he wished he were manning a wrecking-ball. The hour of
pinkish-orange dusk had settled in. We sat for several tense

minutes contemplating the wreckage of the franchise motel, like the prow of a sunken ocean liner breaking the surface of a dead sea.

Manuel hopped out in a display of great haste and walked away several yards. He had extracted a satellite phone from a knapsack, and tapped in a number.

"What's he up to," I demanded of Smith, who held a tiny spoon under his nostrils, re-sampling the bag he'd opened en route.

"Calling in the troops, I imagine," said Smith dreamily. "We'd better decide how much of this shit we want to hang on to before they arrive."

13

"Quite a piquant hamlet you've got here," said Vanessa Savage, rewinding her miniature plastic Godzilla. "I get why they call it Land's End, but why not United Zombies of the British Isles?"

"Title's been taken by Manchester Rugby Team Official Fan Club, I think," said Marco.

Vanessa puffed a Craven A with scabrous scowl and hint of lassitude. She pinned Marco directly by the eyeballs, tossed her auburn tresses.

"It's true I have you to thank for helping me elude Zryd and his fungus of a spouse and the North Korean Girl's Accordion Club," she said. "Though Erna Cuntze played a pivotal role in my escape. God help her if Schnitzelbrotten the Hun ever figures out how I got away. I couldn't've manipulated my way out of there myself with as much deadfaced panache. But now, I learn, you've parked me with a perfectly nice gentleman you expect to detonate himself to smithereens to rid this narcoleptic turdtown of Those That Know, some shadowy little gang that may or may not exist outside your busy, bored imaginations. Have I got that right?"

Khartovski grinned. Fortified by this ebullient but determined creature's militant spirit. He was then seized with a fit of coughing, hawking a wad of sputum against an icon on the wall. It appeared to weep green tears. Marco yawned – a fake yawn, and Vanessa clocked it.

"Well, my laddie, I'm not going to let you send this obviously ill, weary man to the land of 73 virgins before his time, not that there are 73 virgins on the face of the earth or what's left of it at this point and certainly no Inca Stinka paradise in the cosmos where a bunch of seedless grapes await the faithful. Seventy-three seedless grapes, if you have any grasp of literate Arabic. They must be raisins by now if they've been waiting for eternity. Anyway, he's a Marxist, not some fucking anti-Muslamic or kamikaze pouf. And he's coming out of *that* daydream with remarkable rapidity. There are better methods for eliminating unwanted elements of a community than suicide bombing. And besides, community is really stretching the term to its limits in this fractured toilet of a town."

The little Godzilla commenced clip clopping across the table.

"As I piece it together from our Highlander Russian friend here, and bits and pieces I've picked up at that Pooper Scooper excuse for a pub, Those That Know possess some mysterious power over the waking dead condition of the so-called townsfolk during the daytime hours, and this… catalepsy, or just plain fatigue as it's called in any normal place, has been endemic here for over a hundred years."

I admired the way Vanessa Savage summed it all up. Still, I felt no closer to penetrating the mystery than ever. She drummed her manicured, clear-varnished fingernails on the table and set her Godzilla upright after it tipped over again, this time without bothering to wind it up.

"Besides which, you don't even know who Those That Know are. So how'ye planning to detonate them to kingdom come, is what I'd like to know. Has it never occurred to your nimble mind," wondered Vanessa with a saucer-eyed, sardonic air, "that Those That Know may not reside anywhere near Land's End, but know what they know from somewhere quite far away and in a distant country? A place that none of us could possibly suspect? That some emissaries or janissaries or whatever just file reports with them? Maybe Those That Know are in a land so distant that it defies the very idea of distance? After all, you can know all you care to know without observing what you know on a daily basis."

Marco, who, like so many of our friends, thought he knew everything, looked perplexed.

"What do you mean?"

"Just what I said, whatever that was. Oh, yeah, Those That Know. Maybe. Whoever. Now, let's consider this from a different angle than you folk hereabouts have been viewing it."

I, personally, was all ears. I am seldom all talk.

"Number one. Wreck of *The Ardent Somdomite*, carrying a cargo of – of what, does anyone even know *that*?"

Khartovski shook his head while his coughing fit continued.

"Well, let me think," said Marco, making a moue of cogitation, "I'm not a native but I've amassed most of the local lore; I believe the *Ardent* was carrying a cargo of some kind of… mineral or granular substance, a vital ingredient in some primitive form of – chemical weaponry, later developed into mustard gas and used during the First World War."

"Aha!" Vanessa Savage trilled, or sniped, I ought to say, for her voice carried a less feminine range than mere trilling, "NOW we're getting somewhere.

"But we're not getting there fast enough. What IF," she said, ticking off points on her fingertips, "the *Ardent* crew happened to be in the employ of a diabolical HUMAN agent, one who, quite deliberately and cunningly, steered the ship to the guano reefs in order to release the substance into the water table of the local community?"

Khartovski coughed vigorously. He had tuberculosis, as everyone knew, or at least, thought they knew.

"There I think you've worked yourself into a logical corner," countered Marco. "What human agent would himself be immune to the effects of – whatever it was called?"

"Perhaps," trumped Vanessa, "the so-called human being

who invented it might also have invented an antidote, or an immunizing agent. Or wore a gas mask, as far as that's concerned."

She paused. From somewhere in her carry-bag she produced a pair of dice, and began rolling them on the table, playing a private game that amused her.

"Let me share a bit of my personal history with you," she said, standing up and commencing to pace about the room, tossing her ringlets emphatically. "I spent a good bit of my childhood in Shanghai. The truth is, my mother didn't want me. She was an actress, full of ambition, the stage was her life and she wasn't letting any little curly-headed rug rat slow her down. You'd have heard of her, if I cared to mention her name. Met a rather sordid end, and I can't say I'm terribly sorry. Set designer in Finland, last I heard about her. She parked me with my father, and thus began a life of continual shifting about the Far East and the archipelagos and the pit stops of the China trade. He was... well, special to me, of course, as every father is to every little girl, and, frankly, special in some ways I perhaps might have done without the benefit of, but in any event, a bit of a speculating type and a gambling n'er-do-anything who had some close scrapes with the Triads, ultimately paving the path to his own demise, though he did have a period of luck with caraway seeds and betel nuts. I saw quite a lot at a tender age, including the Torment of the Seventeen Blades, right in the streets of the International City. And I kept my eyes and ears open, I can tell you.

"There is an organization that has existed for hundreds if not thousands of years in China. It traffics in opium, in gunpowder, in counterfeit coin and bogus currency, in pleasure girls and slavery, today in nuclear materials and almost any other valuable and controlled substance you care to name. Its stocks in trade of course are gambling proceeds, casinos, even the seemingly harmless, colorful Mah Jong parlors that you see springing up all over London and the world's other cities.

"In China, it has long been known as the FatChowDong, but, more familiarly, the ChoFatDong. It collects the refuse of the human species and… other animate detritus, and puts the criminal element, the will-less, and the evil under its control."

"How do you know so much about it?" Marco, ever the know-it-all, challenged in a perplexed, frustrated manner.

A dust-coated, ornate clock upon the mantlepiece, forever arrested at quarter after twelve, told how time had frozen in Khartovski's adopted village, and how frozen Khartovski had become by adopting it.

"Ha ha, *quelle* question! The ChoFatDong, filth of the earth and masters of the East, murdered my father with the barbaric device known as the Maze of the Twelve Illuminations… each part of his body devoured in stages by starving rats released one cage at a time. And these vicious yellow filth left me to starve in the streets of Shanghai like a Pekinese puppy abandoned by a bored, spoiled Duchess. For weeks I survived on things no girl ought ever have to see, let alone ingest. But my will to survive was stronger than the power of those evil-smelling streets to reduce me to a snack for the pariah dogs and vermin and the child brothels of that vile metropolis. I was rescued by a compassionate silk merchant who taught me the musical art. Specifically the yu, the pinyin, the dongxiao, the nanxiao, and the chiba as well as the Korean tanso, until I had mastered every wind instrument of China.

"And then, to my misfortune, my silk merchant fell to the cholera. Once again I was on my lonesome, but older, and wiser in the ways of the so-called Mystic East. I've been a cigarette girl in a Hong Kong casino and a blackjack dealer in Surabaya. I've played many an instrument and worked many a job in my short but rather exotic life.

"They say," said Vanessa, "and I'm not so certain that they are mistaken, that those who control the ChoFatDong have lived for hundreds of years, that almost all of the organization's original cabal are still alive today, thanks to a discovery made by one of its Eastern European members… an alchemist, so-called, whose daughter, like me, was trained in music, as an opera singer."

Vanessa concluded this recitative with a resigned shrug of her bony shoulders.

"And so, according to you, this ChoFatDong, or FatChowDong, or however you care to call it, is controlled by more than one person?"

Marco strode about Khartovski's parlor as if he owned the place. He didn't like women contradicting him, or telling him anything he didn't know. I had never been certain that he liked women as much as he did womanizing.

"Yes. And no. The principal strategist does not control the organization, but serves as her second-in-command. A woman, perhaps the most diabolical and clever woman the East has ever known, is the *capo di tutti frutti* of the ChoFatDong, but her… emissary, her… accountant, as I like to call him, for lack of a more menial term… for he is, make no mistake, hardly the person in real control – It's he, for it is indeed a him, who was probably aboard the *Ardent* when it hit the reefs – he who, even today, a century later, uses this town as a sort of living experiment, if one calls it living, and, let's face it, they do live it up around here after dark. A laboratory for the study of mind control. He needn't observe the results first-hand… look at this recent mayhem."

Could it be? That we, this place, everything around us, was merely nothing more than a science experiment? What about the violence? Fanny Bacon's killing? Why had some passed on the torpor, while others hadn't? What does the phrase *the law of averages* really mean?

"But what's the purpose of this experiment?" I gasped out the words as best I could, and even though my speech is all but incomprehensible, Vanessa Savage understood me.

"Why, world domination, of course. What other game in town is worth playing?"

14

While Duarte continued his furtive satellite telephone call, Smith and I undertook the removal of several automatic weapons and pistols and roughly seven bags of heroin from the crates they were packed in, having equipped ourselves with spare luggage for this very purpose. Smith hesitated over a nest of Claymore mines in their original excelsior.

"I don't think we have any use for these," he decreed. "Let the FARC or whoever have their fun."

Duarte continued his call while he observed us hauling our luggage into one of the ground-floor rooms facing the parking lot. The door had no lock, and inside, the remains of two twin beds, some smashed-up furniture, a smashed-in television set, and numerous broken lighting fixtures reposed on a litter of torn newspapers, moss, shards of broken glass, and other wreckage, the room a potpourri of foul smells, the source of many of which obviously lay beyond the shut, cracked bathroom door.

Duarte appeared in the doorway.

"I see you've chosen room 14," he nodded. "I was going to advise something on the ground floor. The party you want is in 26, just across the pool and up the stairs."

"I think we'll hold off on our consultation," said Smith drily, "until your friends have come and gone."

Duarte attempted a scandalized expression.

"Surely, Waynuth Snith, you don't think my associates would

confiscate your share of our takings?"

"I have drawn no such conclusion," said Smith. Of course he had. "At the same time, I've no assurance besides your word for it that they wouldn't, and no guarantee that you wouldn't leave Petrie and myself marooned here by roaring off in the Jeep. Let's be candid, Manuel. We have no compelling reason to trust you, or otherwise."

Duarte nodded a manly acknowledgment. This too seemed shrewd, calculated, and insincere.

"Of course you are right, Inspector. In this day and age, an enemy is just a friend you don't know very well."

"Which by no means implies any gross suspicions on my part, I assure you," Smith smoothly lied. "But you'd be cautious under the circumstances too."

"I am being cautious," said Manuel. "For one thing, I'm not going into room 26 with you two, I don't care what kind of shaman he is."

The air fibrillated with a sluicing, buzzing racket that grew louder by the second. As it grew deafening, a black helicopter circled the Holiday Inn sign, churning up a whirlwind of pebbles and sand that pelted the structure and spread clouds of asphyxiating dust across the ruined parking lot, descending with a graceless wobbling flatulence. Once its blades slackened to a detumescent flutter, the open sides of the thing disgorged an unruly-looking gang of perhaps fifteen men in scraggly beards and semi-military khaki shirts and trousers, many of them notably skinny, short, and ill-coordinated, who immediately set about emptying the rear compartment of the Jeep, hauling the loot from the police lockup into the helicopter.

Duarte stepped forward and greeted them effusively, embracing one or two with fervor, exchanging revolutionary pleasantries in Spanish. For a moment he seemed inclined to introduce Weymouth and myself to his *compadres*, but thought better of it. Speed, it appeared, was of the essence: they all seemed to be on it, and once their swag had been tucked aboard, the freedom fighters, or whatever they called themselves, scrambled inside and the giant bug retraced its route.

"Moving west," Smith muttered. "It's the FARC."

The paramilitary team wasted no time before sampling the dope as the helicopter ascended in gales of dust, vast clouds of it suggestive of a nuclear detonation. As Duarte watched the chopper ascend, Smith prudently confiscated the keys from the Jeep's ignition. Blinded by dust, I swiped at my eyelids with a hankie. I now wished I had listened carefully to Weymouth Smith's explanation of the three classes of shaman inhabiting the valley. For we were about to consult with one, or so Smith assured me. Personally, I would not have been surprised if room 26 contained some protoplasmic, carnivorous goo that sucked us up and assimilated us upon opening the door.

But such are the tensions that accompany these fraught, dangerous missions. One's imagination summons nightmarish fantasies. Duarte had helped himself to a hefty snoutful of smack.

"What the hell," he brayed with a swagger, hefting an automatic rifle from under the rear canopy. "I'll go in there too, all for one, one for all." High as the Hubble Telescope, obviously.

"I doubt if we'll be needing that," Weymouth Smith told him, his face disdainful.

"Speak for yourself," Duarte told him sharply.

As we circumnavigated the swimming pool I felt an abnormal quality of silence in that valley of monotonous flora and chutes of sloping granite, the kind of silence that seems to carry not even footfalls, and I believe the darting movement of a small lizard would have startled me out of my wits.

"This unnatural quiet," I said. It was as if my voice never escaped my throat. At any rate, no sound came out.

And then the wind slashed through like a razor slit in an old Silk Cut billboard. The wind fisted down from the granite's natural slides with the savagery of an ocean gale, without warning, hurling tempests of dirt, dust, and dead vegetation from the forest floor across the length and breadth of the Holiday Inn resort area and its surroundings.

Duarte, attempting to shield his face with his gun arm, collapsed to the ground like a bowling pin in a perfect strike. He had been struck on the head with a flying crushed tin of canned tomatoes. The impact was audible.

The swimming pool rapidly filled with sand and muck, crushed cigarette packs, empty tin food cans, small animal corpses, and similar filth; naturally, the parking lot and its periphery were likewise strewn, in places buried, by all the debris thrown down on the wind. The sky had turned a brackish yellow-green color.

Smith and I fought the wind with nothing but our bodies, scrambling for the Jeep: he made immediately for the canopy over the rear body of the vehicle. I followed, trying to protect my eyes. I assumed he felt this would be our best protection and began climbing in.

"No, no, Petrie, you imbecile, secure the ropes! We'll lose all the dope they didn't grab! Look, they left at least twelve bags! Tie her down! Tie her down tightly! Tightly!"

Well, you try it sometime, while being pelted with half-eaten squirrels and clumps of loose, damp earth. Yet Smith, who could never be deterred from anything he perceived as a vital mission, managed not only to egg me on until the rear compartment was, as far as we could tell, storm-proof, but then had enough strength left to pull me, half-dead, into the front seat, which was fully exposed, and really not the best place to be at that moment.

"Just duck and cover," Smith screamed over the howling fury of the storm. "Here, snort something under the dash."

Perhaps he knew more than I did. Perhaps he knew less. Perhaps we were both idiots. And then the howling, angry

winds stopped. Stopped on a dime. Stopped on a penny. Just...
stopped. And the moment they did, the door of room 26 flew
open. A woman stepped out and surveyed the debris field from
the balcony.

I had been led, perhaps by my own wild, terrified imaginings,
to expect a traditional *piya*, or village shaman, to inhabit this
Holiday Inn, as Smith was in quest of information, and only the
piya, of the three classes of shaman of the valley, had established
halfway cordial relations with anthropologists and westerners
generally. Still, my mental image of a shaman, I confess, was
a bit stereotyped and frightful. Not that I actually knew what a
traditional shaman looked like, anyway.

This shaman, if such she was, wore long loose blonde hair,
formfitting grey gaberdine trousers, and a plain blue silk blouse
under a white fringed Western-style jacket.

"You gentlemen lost in the wilderness or something?" she
growled in a tough, Barbara Stanwyck sort of voice. She bore
a distinct resemblance, in fact, to Barbara Stanwyck in "The
Big Valley" – not Barbara's heyday exactly, but not her dotage,
either.

"Not exactly," said Smith. "We're investigating some recent
crimes far, far away from here in a country called England."

"I know where England is, buster. What type of crimes are
you talking about?"

"The kind that involve shape-shifting and metamorphosis...
involuntary transformation of people into insects."

"Insect larva," I corrected him.

"What's that got to do with me?" demanded the Barbara
Stanwyck sound-alike.

"I was told a *piya* lived here."

Her face told a disgusted old story.

"I'm the only *piya* on this ponderosa. Get that through your
cement brain. Haven't had any jelliform hanky-panky in this
quadrant of hell in years. They call me Piya Chiwa but you can

call me Terry. Terry Aden. Studied with Lévi-Strauss at the Sorbonne, Ph.D. from Yale."

Introductions made their rounds. Terry Aden did not favor uninvited drop-ins, it appeared, but prepared to endure our presence, providing it was brief.

"You see how useless it was to put a swimming pool there," she said, gesticulating at the mess in the motel yard. She all but yanked us inside what proved to be an unfolding suite of exquisitely appointed rooms full of polished, frameless mirrors and Ikea furniture, electronics equipment, a virtual Command Center of some sort.

"We should tend to Duarte," I said half-heartedly, the medical man in me recrudescing after the meteorological shocks I'd experienced.

"If you mean the *amigo* with his left nostril packed with white powder – I've got eyesight like a raptor, gentlemen – he's moved on."

"Moved on? Where's there for him to move on to?"

"He's passed over."

"Passed over the bridge? The Green Bridge that led us to this remote spot?"

That bridge. I wouldn't have crossed it for a year's supply. Duarte had wanted to roar across it in the Jeep, delusional arsehole that he was.

"Penetrated the veil, my friend," said Terry Aden, or Piya Chiwa, with a perfunctory nod of her chin. "Looked like a bad 'un, anyways."

Smith, whose acuity was matched at times by his density, pressed the matter like a schnauzer with a marrow bone.

"Veil? Is that what's called hereabouts the shroud of mist that sometimes envelopes hillside valleys such as this one?"

Terry Aden glanced at her watch. Smith had succeeded in boring her stiff in record time. She poured herself a short brandy and tossed it back.

"He's checked out of this Holiday Inn, let's put it that way, and left you two holding the bags."

Thank god, I thought, he didn't steal the dope from our room. But then, I knew he'd done no such thing.

"Shit, did he hot-wire the Jeep?"

Had Smith simply ambled out of room 26 and gandered over the balcony, he would have seen the Jeep parked where we'd left it. He'd also have seen that passing over the bridge and passing through the veil amounted to the same thing.

"Doesn't need a Jeep where he's going, which is nowhere special. He's dead. Look, Inspector Smith, I've about run out of euphemisms and I assume you didn't come from 'a country called England' to waste my time and yours on inane banter."

Smith looked absurdly Victorian. He blushed, or very nearly.

"Dead? How's that even possible? He was alive less than ten minutes ago."

An even more absurd utterance. I think Terry Aden stimulated his kundalini against his will. She definitely did mine.

"Ten seconds can be an eternity, or a ticket out to it," sighed Piya Chiwa Terry Aden. "Back then – and it is 'back then,' y'know – his frontal lobes hadn't collided at sixty miles per hour with a sharp-edged, discarded Del Monte jumbo-sized can of crushed tomatoes, in the rough shape of an Aztec adze, which would be my guess as to cause of… death, if we can cut to the chase here."

Manuel Duarte, R.I.P. Good riddance to bad rubbish, to speak ill of the departed.

"Good grief, Smith," I said, playing my role as dumbo side-kick. Fiction can be stranger than fact. An adze can be a deadly weapon, as everyone knows. "Killed by a can of tomatoes."

"And an empty can, too," Smith wonderingly exclaimed. "Who'd have imagined such an unlikely end to our *compadre*?"

I didn't find Duarte's end all that unlikely, though I suppose I'd have given better odds on execution by the same comrades who'd materialized in the helicopter. To his credit, Smith had already relinquished any sentimental enlargement on the topic of Manuel Duarte, who hadn't been such sparkling company in the first place.

"The sands will take him. Soon all trace of him will be gone with the winds. You see," said Terry Aden Piya Chiwa, pouring herself another brandy from what I believe is called a "wet bar," "those swine who inhabit the middle plateau, these so-called alleluia-san, are superstitiously held to be heavenly singers whose choruses ward off the kanaimà evil. Bunch of fairies, I've always said. Slobs, too. Throw their garbage everywhere. They scavenge canned food in Georgetown, scurry back to the ravines with it, and toss the mess just anywhere in the once-pristine forest. They also pilfer scrap iron from the *favelas* to build ridiculous lean-to shelters. They've pretty much wrecked an ecological paradise. You name it, in a stiff wind this place gets clobbered with it – Dole, Del Monte, Goya – oh, boya – and other tinned food, when real food is, or anyway was, plentiful, simply by reaching up into fruit-laden tropical trees of ancient origin! But like the morons they are, they've chopped down half of those fecund ecological miracles for firewood and cattle grazing. Soon the valley will be no more a valley than… Lankershim Boulevard.

"And, despite the hankering they obviously have to see McDonald's Golden Arches pulsing puke yellow parabolas into the night's oblivion, they are primitive enough to resist electrification. So our nights here are pitch black, now that the generator is the rusting hulk of scrap metal out in what used to be the tennis court. And they wonder why the kanaimà multiply and continue their unspeakable practices.

"Or, I should say – whiskey, gentlemen? – *did* continue. Until yours truly arrived with my team of crack enforcement agents. They're out nabbing woolly bullies as we speak. We've rounded up a fair percentage of these rotten corpse-sucking psychotics, whose practices – excuse me, I just finished lunch, I'd prefer not to go into detail."

She didn't seem the reflux type, so I assumed she simply found the topic old hat.

"Terry – " said Smith.

The mirrored room multiplied our images into infinity, like the walls of certain swanky restaurant bathrooms. I saw myself as others saw me: a well-meaning, absent-minded middle-aged party, dressed in the depth of fashion.

"Piya Chiwa, if you prefer. I personally don't."

Terry Aden strode purposefully to a wall mirror and reapplied a rust shade of lipstick, smacked her lips, began feathering her eyelashes with mascara. Not for us, I had the feeling.

"What do you do with them when you apprehend these kanaimà?"

She scowled, testing the effect of her makeup, at Smith's habitual, cheeky, interrogating tone. None of your goddam business, her eyes told him in reflection. She wandered to the piano and sat at the keyboard, sight-reading a piece by Brahms.

"Indirectly, up 'til now, we've underwritten our research facility with them. Oh, a few still stalk the hills and perform their… ritual stalkings and the rest of their bloodthirsty horseshit. Can't clean up the whole country, and they're not just in Guyana, you know.

"Directly beneath where we're currently lounging, there's a ward of lockdown cells based on the state-of-the-art California prison system in Atascadero, where about ten of these 'shamans' are compulsively masturbating and flinging their excrement into each other's cells, yearning for god knows what besides food, and god, who cares. They get two squares a day. Doesn't do to keep them too hardy. Then…."

Piya Chiwa hesitated, like Barbara Stanwyck in *The Strange Love of Martha Ivers* hesitates before revealing the full scope of her own culpability in the staircase murder of her guardian aunt.

Terry, however, wasn't haunted by herself as Barbara Stanwyck had been, but dismayed at the thought kanaimà would continue to roam the earth.

"I sense some hesitation on your part," said Inspector Smith, which really was a superfluous observation. Something of a specialty with Smith, if truth be told.

"Because it's no skin off your arse what we do with them, frankly, so I wonder why I'm telling you. You know funding for all kinds of scientific research has dried up in these dark times. We have to take our operating budget where we can scrape it together. And, take my word for it, these kanaimà practitioners are not fully human, or, if they are, we really need a new qualifying adjective for what they are. Anyway, we hold them in our makeshift tank, remove them from the denser tribal areas, underfeed them enough to keep them a little anemic, and, once every three or four weeks, a Hummer fleet crosses the wasteland the lowlanders have made from the foothills, out there, and an entrepreneur, who arrives always at night, and whose name I don't know… well, he takes them off our hands."

"Incarcerates them?"

"Well, certainly, but he's not Johnny Law, so I assume he's buying them for his own researches."

"You *sell* human beings?" Smith said with professional disapproval. My experience in the opiate trade hardly afforded me such indignation.

"I've told you before," Terry Aden said peevishly, "they are not what we can consider human beings. They're a bad science experiment of our species, like most people, only too extreme in their habits to let rummage about loose. Once they are kanaimà, they become… in their own minds, but furthermore in the minds of their human prey, shape-shifters, leopards, all sorts of wildlife, anything but human."

What *is* human, I wondered. The concept of personhood I understood, but *human* had so many negative associations in my mind that I could award it few unqualified accolades.

"Who? Who? Who has any use for these... cannibal kanaimà?"

Smith now studied his own reflected image. He seemed to dislike what he saw, and something verging on introspection worried at his frownies.

"Really, Inspector Smith, you sound like an owl. If you plan to keep on like one, kindly don't start dropping pellets and the feathers of your prey on my carpet. That's an heirloom you're standing on. *Cannibal* is a mild term for what these reptilian brains have evolved as a method of killing and feasting on their victims."

She seemed to recall what Smith and myself purportedly were doing there, and decided to toss us a helpful bone.

"Some Oriental walking skeleton with a pigtail and long fingernails and his bodyguards, who look to me like Nubian hairdressers, only sort of ash-colored instead of black. Not fairies exactly, but celibates, assuredly.

"They're... I don't know. Grey, would be the color I'd pick. Slightly lighter grey than my slacks. Ash grey, corpselike, take your pick. They restrain the kanaimà in straight jackets, pack them in a refrigerator compartment with a lot of dangling pig carcasses, and rumble back out of the valley.

"We've needed the revenue to keep this place going, getting our data, interviewing the locals. Now, however, we're closing down the whole facility. Nothing more to be gleaned from these primitive imbeciles except what you find in some academic footnotes by third-rate armchair anthropologists.

"I study kinship systems, not wig-whack tribal superstitions. My work is done among these... ugh. I mean really, like I said in the first place. Bunch of big fairies. Sing tuneless songs all day, cower in fear, and crap up the rain forest with their garbage all night. Not much of a life, is it? Let Mel Gibson have wet dreams about it."

She awaited someone's arrival. She evidently wished us out of there before that person materialized.

"But it's… it's *immoral*!"

Terry Aden studied her profile in the mirrored wall, made a few adjustments to her ensemble.

"Closing down a half-demolished motel nobody's operated for nine years? What's immoral about that? Slum clearance if you ask me. With any luck, the jungle will swallow this whole place in six months."

Now, she signalled to me, will you folks kindly be on your way?

"The sales, the disposal of the kanaimà!"

"Oh, piffle," said Terry, plunking a few keys on the badly tuned upright piano under a portrait of some long-ago Guyanese dictator. "Ever come face to face with one of these shit-for-brains? Not a pretty picture."

She attempted a short passage of Brahms, but the piano sounded wretchedly atonal. She lifted her fingers from the keys and pointed at Smith.

"And, morally speaking, as you seem to like doing, don't tell me everything you do in your, uh, police work is on the up-and-up, Inspector. Believe it or not, stories about you have reached us even here in this… *garden of earthly ruination*."

She hissed out the words. Smith, oblivious to her impatience, made me eager to skedaddle.

"But it's tantamount to slavery!" Smith sputtered.

Terry yawned. Glanced again at her watch.

"Tantamount. In my dictionary, that means equal in value. Not a well-chosen word, Smith. Equal to what, nuclear warfare? Drive-by gang killings? What happens after those Hummers pull out has never tweaked my imagination. Neither will this place, as of a week from Tuesday. We're airlifting out the valuable stuff, all the data, and, paltry piffle it may seem to you, what we've managed to collect, science will thank us for in the future. Maybe in the present, though I don't have eyes on any Nobel Prize. I'd rather be eating ice cream, frankly. We're taking the furniture, too, so don't get any ideas. Dr. Petrie, you look like you need… perhaps something you left in that room across the pool?"

I needed it more than ever. A spike in the vein, an orchid blooming in the brain.

"I'll get you a spoon from the model kitchen Ikea donated when we opened this facility," Terry offered brightly. "I expect you need a cotton ball or two as well, maybe some alcohol? And you can borrow my lighter. Return it, please. It's the last working Bic in the valley."

Weymouth Smith's mug was a rictus of conflict: yes, he was a loyal inspector of Scotland Yard. No, he didn't give a shit what happened to these kanaimà any more than I did, except that… the Chinese part smacked, no pun intended, of… yes, the wily, the diabolical, the brilliant, the indomitable, the unceasingly inventive foe of the white race… you know who.

"If it's any help to you boys," Terry said brightly, returning in a fetching outfit of white leather trousers and a beige jacket, holding an heirloom soup spoon out to my greedy fingers, "they forgot to strip the plates off a Hummer on one occasion. Paraguayan. So, maybe they drive them all the way down to the landlocked haven of Nazi filth. I wouldn't know. Good place for them, though. That's one country that gives even me the shudders."

A jagged piece of the puzzle clicked into place. But I was busy dashing down to my conscience-easing substance before I could hear whatever dialogue followed between the bogus *piwa* shaman, a woman who really knew what time it was, and Inspector Smith, who really didn't, if you ask me.

15

Fu Manchu nuzzled the adorable, snarling Cutie under the chin, puffing at his impossibly long opium pipe. His sibilance murmured into the speaker phone, again on the blower to Roswitha Klebb, his evanescent voice imperturbable and higher, in the drugged sense, than she'd ever heard it.

"Well, well, Klebb, wouldn't you know it, that lazy-ass Ken Jay, terrified for his precious little offspring – talk about a dry hole, that little bitch has given me more headaches than I can count, anyway, they'll both be disposed of in a few days – came through ahead of schedule with the mutations and they're ready for use once we get the transmitters glued to their... antennae feelers."

"I told you so," Roswitha told him so. "Just threaten the daughter with burrowing centipedes, maybe the old Zaybar Kiss, makes their brains spin faster than a cyclotron. Why, back in my STASI days – "

"Yes, yes, you are always right, Klebb, and I, mere immortal Fu Manchu, proud visionary of the destruction of the white race and its so-called civilization, as per usual, am always wrong. But: have those pissant Muslims come across with the swag?"

"Thought you cottoned to the towel-head sand niggers," said Klebb. She watched as Oduvaldo attempted to squirm his way out of a confrontation with Sibelia. Sibelia had discovered the card of a disreputable night club in one of his jackets while emptying its pockets to send to the dry cleaner. Outside, the sky over Ciudad del Este had turned mint green and urine yellow. Klebb found her favorite Mama Cass muumuu now fit her, one of the day's more encouraging signs.

"When they're of any *financial use*," said Fu, dreamily. "I have no love of the barbaric Islamics. I shall dispose of them too after they pay up."

Klebb, soaking her deformed foot in a so-called herbal bath of Dead Sea Salts while keeping some carjacking employees on hold, told him excitedly: "Guess what, right after we last spoke, Abu Pinochle or whatever his name is turned up with a suitcase full of diamonds. I'm having them appraised before turning over the spent fuel rods and the encased liquids. I wouldn't put it past them to slip a zircon or two into the mix."

"Oh, Klebb, always complicating everything."

"Look who's talking. The original can of worms. First you want to eliminate Weymouth Smith, then you send him a luxury gift package in the form of a clue."

"PLUS! A brand new shipment of five kanaimà!"

Roswitha's groan could be heard above the traffic in the street below.

"Don't imagine for one second you're shipping those – ghouls over here."

She'd seen some of them in the streets of Ciudad del Este, right out in broad daylight. They unnerved her. They were practically transparent, like Handi-Wrap.

"No no no no NO, of course not. Our plans for our disemboweling and corpse-sucking friends are a whole other bucket of fishbait. Non-essential elements, but useful for terrorizing London, or some parts of it anyway.

"Don't think I'm not keeping your welfare in mind. You'll be busy escorting the Cold Children to England when I test the Neutron Dissembling Device on Ciudad del Este. Should make most of those mosques and pawn shops disintegrate into their component particles. Oh, don't worry your ugly little foot, I mean head, my dear, you'll be safe and sound, in flight to the airport in Manchester."

Klebb, intent on reading Sibelia's lips in Portugese, only caught his gist on the fly, so to speak.

"WHAT???"

She abhorred those Cold Children almost as much as the kanaimà shamen. Horrid little monsters from beyond the grave. The STASI had been such a straightforward organization by comparison. Everything with Fu turned out byzantine and overcomplicated. Klebb enjoyed a bit of that, but a little ran a long way.

"I never explained the master plan? Oh, Roswitha, I think you're hitting the joyful powder a bit too joyfully these days."

One day, she thought, this joker's hubris will lead him to a stony end. Uglier than I am, and I'm no slouch. She straightened her posture to reinforce this idea for herself.

"I have been clean as a whistle for at least four weeks," Roswitha snarled. She attempted to count back the days. "Just chipping now and again. To kill the pain, you know. I'm not a recreational user any more. I even go to the meetings. Have to liquidate the other N/A sharers afterwards, of course, so I have to vary the meeting places every time. You pick up some interesting stories in that room. Sometimes I feel a little sad they have to die right after they spill their guts. Of course, *you* don't feel pain, we all know that."

It's true, she marvelled. Fu feels no pain. Who does on all that opium? You could drag him over broken glass by the geriatric balls with piano wire and he'd just keep on dreaming the dream.

"It pains me to no end when my minions forget their submissive mission, their enslavement to my will. I'm quite sure I informed you these youngsters need a chaperone to get through all the security obstacles this new set of immigration laws have tossed in the path of freedom of movement since 9/11. I've written it in my day book."

Klebb had quite forgotten whether 9/11 was a cop show or the emergency number you dialed in New York City. 9/11, 9/11… now it would haunt her until she pinpointed what it was. Unless she took a little poke from the storage room. *It's working, it's working, keep working* – she forgot the rest of the N/A chant. Something about every day being a new day.

Every day, Klebb thought, is all the same fucking day.

"As if I had freedom of movement to begin with. Look, Fu, I bet these children of the damned look… really creepy, am I right? Spooky? Pale? Like that George Saunders movie? With eyes that light up in the dark? They've been dead once, how do you imagine they're gonna get out of Paraguay without a complete set of shots from a veterinarian? Don't they still quarantine animals in England?"

She loathed travel. She loathed small children. Especially dead ones. As if she didn't have enough on her hands. She had, in fact, two Wesson-oiled fingers deep in her twat, awaiting Oduvaldo's reappearance on the plasma screen. She knew he had a long scene coming up.

"They're *children*, for god's sake, where's your humanity?"

He's becoming a Pez dispenser of homilies, thought Klebb. Losing his grip. Maybe MI5 would take her back if she spilled what she knew. Anyway, Fu was a monster. Not one like her, one like him. She'd met them all, and Fu really took the cake, whipped cream topping and maraschino cherries included.

"Humanity," she snorted. "Don't give me 'humanity' at this hour."

He sounds just like Lillian Hellman, she told herself. Just like that old cabbage in the Blackglama ad. She'd bet anything he had his glazed eyes fixed on the telenova too. It had everything: murder, incest, mental retardation, adultery, money.

And swanky residences, upscale office furnishings, the works.

"Once unleashed, along with Ken Jay's latest creations, Great Britain will hardly call itself Great any longer, I can assure you. Britain, maybe, if the population of sleepwalkers we shall create wish to retain the old moniker, which I doubt. If the Land's End Long Range Study has any value whatever, if it's proven anything, it's the intrinsic weakness of the white race – present company on the phone excepted and of course your Teutonic ancestors."

Roswitha Klebb had long concealed her Polish origins from her employers – the East Germans, the Brits, Saks during the Christmas season, and her current Asian master: all these maniacs except Saks had a thing against "polocks." She felt a stirring of revolt against his generalizations. We had Chopin, she proudly ruminated, we had Gombrowicz, we had *Quo Vadis* – and these twin brothers as presidents, that was a twist on international politics nobody'd thought of. We even had Lithuania for a long time.

"But Fu – what about Phase Three? We haven't even gotten Phase Three underway yet. And you said that Phase Three was vital before launching the bugs and the… all right, I won't call them animals, but whatever those kids are."

Fu Manchu chuckled through the haze of opium surrounding his inscrutable and ravaged ancient face.

"Oh, Klebb, you've been so preoccupied with your fuel rods and bootleg Marlboros, you forgot to check the launch of Phase Three on your wall calendar. It is well underway already. Phase Three *is* the insects. I mean *are* the insects. All in due time, my princess of diabolism!"

Comparing me to him. Thinks it's a compliment. No, she concluded, he's losing it, finally. Really losing it. That serum has to have some expiration date on it.

"Princess, my ass. Clubfoot Annie behind my back, I'd be willing to bet on it."

"But in China, Klebb, your deformed foot would be regarded as an object of extreme erotic allure!"

"And in Paraguay," snapped Klebb, "I'm gaped at as another freaky fat cripple."

Oh, god, these interminable sniping exchanges, thinks Fu, when there's serious business afoot. Or rather at hand. He now wonders if… Klebb drinks a little, since kicking her opium habit, if she actually has.

16

The morning after I met Vanessa Savage, two conventionally suited commercial travellers sat in close proximity, on lounge chairs in the Queen Edward Hotel lobby in Pincer Street reading newspapers. That is, to all appearances.

The night clerk, an obese, effeminate, and imposingly large party named Paulie Andros, had concluded his shift two hours earlier, and the day man, a mustached and proper old desiccation, much given to snuffling as though his nasal passages were afflicted with incipient snot, known only as Mr. Higgins, remarkable solely for the scarred pentimento of a deep ovoid gash in his upper left forehead, stood stationed at his post near the mailbox and keyring cabinet, himself immersed in the morning's Racing Form.

Mr. Higgins was an incurious man, a man about whom no one had ever given a first, let alone second, thought, so perfectly did he coincide with the image of a hotel desk clerk "of a certain age." He was a man of bland habits, married to a bland woman, with a brood of bland children at home, which was somewhere in the upper town. His forehead wound, decades old, had been self-inflicted: as a younger man, he had appreciated life's meaninglessness and attempted to sever the lobes of his brain with a samurai sword acquired at a martial arts supply store, in hopes of producing two distinct persons, one of whom might find some reason for continuing to exist. But such dreams no longer troubled his sleep, and the scar, on the rare occasion when he glimpsed himself in a mirror, no longer even summoned this adolescent canard to his memory. He seemed to recall being bitten on the head by some large animal, or at least that was how he now accounted for it to himself. Higgins worked his shift, finished his shift, and, as far as anyone might note, including Higgins himself, ceased to exist until his following shift.

Therefore, it took a considerable time for Higgins to observe the unusual immobility of these transient salesmen behind their copies of, respectively, *The Times* and *The Observer*. And it may well have taken hours for Higgins to make that discovery, had not a telephone call for one of them broken the stasis of that drowsy lobby.

Yet when Higgins called to Mr. Daley, as his name was, according to the Queen Edward Hotel register, and received no reply, he came out from behind the front desk and approached the fellow, who remained unresponsive to his increasingly strident beckoning. It was after Higgins found it necessary to give the individual a perfunctory tap on his shoulder, along with his neighbor's, as he could not tell which was whom, that Mr. Daley's head fell off his body, followed immediately by that of the man seated beside him, a Mr. Brolindale.

A bloody mess upon the pages of both newspapers soon enough told a sorry tale.

Both had been cleanly decapitated by some razor sharp implement, to all appearances, and, after being disturbed, now sat with their heads in their newspaper-covered laps, literally, their necks still upright, a sight which sent the otherwise impervious Higgins into a state of utter hysteria.

The Land's End police, summoned frantically, declared themselves utterly stumped, not to be literal-minded, by this ghastly vision, two respectable-looking men in business suits whose heads had been cleanly separated from their bodies and remounted in their previous locations, for as far as anyone knew, the men enjoyed no acquaintance with each other, had arrived at the hotel hours separately, and, obviously, enjoyed no connection with each other now, except as victims in a ghastly crime which, being deceased, neither was aware of.

An urgent call to Scotland Yard brought the professionals to the scene in a cacophony of sirens which was a gratuity common to such emergency personnel, especially since the possibility of resuscitation of either decapitee was nil. The crime scene, duly dusted for fingerprints, laboriously scoured everywhere for clues, was examined minutely for anything which would indicate telling information about these ghastly homicides.

That very afternoon, the dismembered body of Lady Eleanor Parkinson-Taylor floated in greater than normal obesity to the surface of a brackish canal that ran, or more accurately, sluggishly slogged along, being clogged with all manner of sewage, behind a cohort of exceptionally squalid drinking establishments along Gin Lane.

Nor had the day's horrors fully unfolded. Another of the town's familiar Ladies of Pleasure, Meg Pegtoroth, never recently seen without a cloche hat to conceal the baldness resulting from chemotherapy, was discovered hanging, upside down, her hat missing from her hairless head, from the topmost turret window of Finester Chateau, once a popular tourist destination, on the westernly outskirts of Land's End. Her neck had been slashed open, her tongue pulled out of her mouth and made to extrude from the resultant gash. A Goodyear radial tire had been hung around Meg Pegtoroth's neck and some attempt had been made to set it ablaze, but whatever accelerant her assailant had employed had proven inadequate to fully incinerate her, merely creating a stench of burning rubber that spread for at least a quarter mile in every direction.

And thus what later became known in law enforcement circles as the Land's End Dead Awakening had moved, so to speak, into high gear.

17

"NOW they'll start tasting the fear!" exulted Fu Manchu.

Sorry to report, still Petrie here. Without pointing an accusing finger at Weymouth Smith, who could not, despite his chess master's perspicacity, have intuited the trap we had been diabolically led into, both he and I were now enchained to incredibly weighty iron chairs, face-to-face across a dungeonlike room, at a distance which taunted with nearness yet fell short of our ability to make tactile contact to aid each other's bondage.

Fu Manchu's voice reached us from the thickly barred window high on the heavy metal door of this death chamber (for so it indubitably seemed to be): he addressed an unseen presence in what I presumed was an outer corridor of some sort. This barrier's barred window admitted the only light that prevented us from sitting in total darkness.

"We'll never get these shackles off," Weymouth Smith griped with a flummoxed tone. "Unless – "

His voice broke off. Whatever eureka he had hoped to astound me with had failed to make its way into his consciousness. I refrained from filling the ensuing silence with "unless what?" because I knew such *unlesses*, unless he really had one to follow up with, were mere wounds to Smith's fragile ego boundaries.

"Tell me, Smith," I said instead, with forced joviality. "Do you imagine there's a chance Proletariat will win the Derby for a third time in a row this year?"

"Impossible," Smith snapped.

"I'm unaware of any strong contenders," I said.

"No, I meant, impossible that such an impasse could present itself again, as it has many times in the past, Petrie – of course, this is your first real direct experience of Dr. Fu Manchu."

Strange to say, I still hadn't had any direct experience with Fu Manchu, only his half-breed slaves.

"Apparently my first and last, Smith."

I should've stayed home, I thought. But what a dreary prospect. Same hangers-on, same bunch of patients with imaginary ailments, and worse still the ones with real ones.

"Every dog has its day," said Smith. "Perhaps mine has been overdue. I have often pondered that the great doctor has, on many occasions, spared me at the last minute, from motives I could never fathom."

Thanks for counting me in, asshole. But, what had I expected? Intrigue, danger, and Smith's unbelievable self-absorption.

"Yes, well, all well and good, but what about me? What have I done to deserve being chained like a monkey to these strange clumps of metal furniture – "

"AHA!" Smith ejaculated.

"Nothing aha about it from my perspective," I said. "More like, aaah, shit!"

I had found my voice at last. Now I could tell him the truth about himself. But what was the truth about Weymouth Smith? I'd never really known, and I supposed I never really would. I still don't, to this day.

"And yet you just provided the exact way in which we may be able to free ourselves from our bondage."

"How would that be, Smith?"

"By your use of the word *monkey* – now, mind you, I know my upper mammals and I fully realize that a marmoset is not, strictly speaking, a monkey. I mean it is a monkey, but not the common mental picture we summon as a monkey. They have prehensile hands and feet, and so on – "

"Somehow we must entice the marmoset into this dungeon carrying the keys to our shackles as well as the key to that thirty-ton door," I finished for him. "If that's where you were going with that inspiration, Smith, I should like to know, for starters, how you plan to make… our pleas audible to this so-called Cutie without alerting Fu Manchu, first of all. Second, how you will entice a marmoset to obtain a set of keys which are, no doubt, kept on a thick round metal keyring, and, third – "

Yet before I could get to third, something unanticipated occurred.

The heavy door began moving. It began moving open inwardly – I don't mean that it had movements inside itself, or had any quality of "inwardness" – oh god, I'm getting as nuts as Smith with statements like that – what I mean to write is, *the door began to creak open.*

I suppose it wasn't as heavy a door as it looked, since the creature who opened it was lithe, slender, about five-feet-six-inches in height, had flowing brownish hair secured at the nape with a crimson ribbon, and was, unmistakably, female: the most beautiful woman I had ever glimpsed.

She quickly shut the door behind her.

"We must be very swift," said her silken voice. Her skin was slightly bosky in hue, suggestive of a Eurasian parentage.

Her hand gripped a massive keyring. She knelt before me and instantly tried key after key on my ankle restraints.

"My name," whispered this ethereal apparition, "is Lilah."

She inserted one after another of a myriad of large, heavy keys looped into the keyring. I could not take my eyes off those perfectly inscribed, crystalline features, those amethyst eyes, as Lilah struggled with the keys.

It was the face I had dreamed on the plane, that I had thought I'd hallucinated while on the nod.

"My name is Obregon," I murmured.

She gazed into my face. Our eyes locked in a kind of ocular embrace.

"And what about ME?" Smith protested, restive in his immobilizing restraints.

Lilah pretended not to hear him, or ignored him, agitatedly fumbling with the oversized keys, finding none that matched my shackles. A faint, rustling movement in the hall's distant depths reached our ears.

"It's too late. Fu Manchu, or his cadre of bodyguards, will appear at any moment."

Something small and metallic pressured into my shackled hand.

"Listen carefully, for the sake of your very lives. And of mine. The object you're holding is a device that's not been approved for the market. It's called an iMe2. There is a wafer-thin slide compartment on the back where the regular iMe contains a battery.

"In it you will find two things: first, a supply of fifteen miniature but extremely potent loop needles. Second, a tubular device I obtained which functions as a blowgun. Observe, Dr. Petrie – Obregon – I'm pre-arming it for you with a loop needle.

"Whomever next enters will be intent on eliminating you. You must accurately disable this individual, and then press this yellow button on the console.

"That will enable you to do what is called a walk-in on the victim's psyche, supplanting it with your own mind and will. Your body will remain shackled to this chair – but, as you'll then control the individual you've looped, inhabiting his body and mind, if it is a male, most likely it will be, you can command it to follow whatever actions your will dictates.

"There isn't time to acquaint you with all the features of the iMe2. It is, unless you're familiar with the facing keyboard, counter-intuitive in design, so I strongly advise you not to attempt to operate its other functions. Except one.

"The green button activates a neuro-interference software interface that allows you, not merely to vacate another person's sensorium and enter it, but to modify certain characteristics, not only of their psyche, but your own physical appearance – in other words, you'll inhabit, for however long you've programmed it for – I've preset it for exactly one hour – the other person's mind and body, but your own as well. It can modify, rather dramatically, the musculature, body type, and bone structure you possess, transfiguring it into a more convenient one. My advice is simple: a menu will appear on this iMe2 ID screen. You will want to become an ectomorph whose extremities easily slide from the shackles.

"Of course you can compel the loop victim approaching to liberate you, and unshackle both yourself and Inspector Smith. But depending on the time setting, you will need also to imprison your jailers in the same manner that restrains you now. I hardly need to tell you they are not the ectomorphic type, but these restraints are adjustable.

"One more caveat: unlikely as it is, if it is Fu himself who appears in here, you must deploy the loop needle precisely where it will have its sole efficacy. Namely one of his eyeballs, reaching through his optical nerve and penetrating his frontal lobes. Even Fu is not immune to this technology, though his powerful mind will not succumb for very long."

"But Lilah – what about yourself? You're imprisoned here I assume, or you wouldn't be helping us now – how will we find you?"

"I shall be far away, Petrie. My father has devised a rather unconventional means of escape for both of us, and doubt not, Petrie. We shall meet again. Don't know where, don't know when. But I know we'll meet again some sunny day."

And with that Lilah slipped quickly out the door, concealing the keyring in the folds of her elaborately decorated kimono.

Smith, strangely quiet, now said, in a chastened voice: "Deucedly clever, that girl. And if I'm not mistaken, fondly taken with you."

We had, of course, made a bee-line for Paraguay after the information imparted by Terry Aden. Paraguay, as Bette Davis remarked of old age, isn't for sissies. We arrived at Asunción expecting who knows what to reveal itself. Yet something did, largely thanks to Smith's acute deductive reasoning, which had sobered itself in light of the less than perspicacious conclusions he'd recently been leaping to, and a fortifying shot of B12.

"I'm not intimately familiar with this burg," Smith admitted. "I do know the upper city is pretty hairy at night and seething with hostility towards strangers during the day. But just below the hill, if you discount what they call, after nightfall, Cutthroat Park, and ply a bit to the west, there's an affluent zone of immaculately tree-lined sidewalks where the most securely ensconced Klaus Barbie types maintain their villas, working on their elaborate memoirs of self-exculpation and denial. My senses tell me that somewhere amid that Germanic, jumped-up trash we may turn up a useful lead."

The lead we discovered, alas, was precisely the one least likely to prove helpful from a personal health perspective: an evidently deserted chateau, entirely dark, several of its narrow windows cracked, with many architectural excrescences that could plausibly contain hidden passageways, secret rooms, or oubliettes in the flooring. A mere thirty yards separate from what seemed a veritable *palais de jamais* through the slatted window blinds and gauzy curtains of which a great deal of inchoate activity occupied an unusual number of unidentifiable persons, including one wing which, I surmised, contained some species of scientific laboratory, judging from the strong fluorescent lighting which banks in the ceiling cast on gleaming metal surfaces and what appeared to be glass beakers, cages or containers of some stripe, and a peripatetic figure wearing a white smock.

"Dollars to doughnuts," Smith mused, "whatever that phrase is supposed to mean, that hive-like sugar shack across the thatch grass is the abode, or one of them, of our arch-enemy, whatever that means. Granted, he has a markedly arch side to his personality."

"By Lagerfeld's Jovan, Smith, I cannot avoid thinking you're right, despite the excessive time I spend thinking that you're wrong."

How to proceed? I shall trust the reader has read the novel *Absalom, Absalom!* by the immortal William Faulkner, and surmised that our plans inevitably led to ingress into the aforesaid edifice of cyanodic gingerbread by way of the neighboring ruin. Moreover, the pitch dark pile of decrepitude we had wordlessly agreed to enter as an observation post contained enough decayed flooring, decrepit staircases, and other miserabilia to send even a person with perfect eyesight, such as Piwa Chiwa Terry Aden, ass-over-bandbox if he or she ventured blindly forward inside, or even with the aid of a candle or a battery torch.

It was only midday, and little threat to visibility outside – but who knew how much sunlight penetrated those narrow windows, whether they were boarded up inside, how much dust and grime sullied the interior, et cetera?

In a trice, whatever that means, Smith and I had jimmied open a rear service door, into what had once been a kitchen, one formerly staffed by a full complement of servants. There was even a dumb-waiter, a gas stove of pre-Cambrian vintage, a sink containing nothing apart from a lonesome millipede and a potato bug, cracked linoleum tiles of a color I would hesitate to describe with hope of accuracy, though they were embellished with a floral design of faintest pink, a breakfront surprisingly stocked with Spode and other upscale dishware, and, dangling from a screwed-in hook above an abnormally long and narrow window above the sink, a shrunken human head.

There had been a craze for such obscene touches of interior décor among Britain's hoi-polloi in the far-off past, both before and after the heavily expurgated report of the noble-minded, valiant Irish patriot (and recipient of the British OBE), Roger Casement, detailing the atrocities perpetrated on the Congolese aboriginals ruled by King Leopold of Belgium. The rapacity of the colonials exceeded the imagination of the Aztecs and would have made an SS unit blush, or perhaps turn iridescent green with envy.

The "reforms" following Casement's heavily expurgated report left the vicious regent of that pisspot nation – I refer to Belgium, the Congo was rich in rubber by comparison – in control of the territory where rampant savagery by Europeans and their loyal colonial subjects was imputed to a rubber consortium which, in reality, acted primarily for Leopold's enrichment. The shrunken-head fad faded, but enjoyed an exultant renaissance in the Putumayo region of Peru, both before and after Casement's subsequent investigation of atrocities committed upon rubber harvesters there by a British-owned company, in collusion with both the Peruvian and Colombian nations, which both laid claim to the Putumayo territory.

Casement had pricked an overinflated balloon, a realm where, as photographic documents amply reflect, "transgressors" resisting the draconian slave labor regime were routinely relieved of hands, feet, limbs, noses, lips, eyelids, ears, and heads. We can see their jubilant fellow slaves, loyal to the colonial authorities, carrying these trophies by the hair. The world since that ever-retreating historical time has merely elaborated a plethora of novel methods of torture, mutilation, rape, pillage, dismemberment, and the dumping of bodies into mass graves, from one end of the planet to another. One could almost regard the barbarities recorded by Roger Casement as mere walk-through rehearsals for the destruction of civilization that lay ahead.

Casement's own conviction for treason – surreptitiously fortified by the circulation of his so-called "Black Diaries" alleged to earmark carnal liaisons with natives of the Putumayo, with Congolese youths, with English and Irish lads well past the prevailing age of consent – cast his heroic humanitarian labors in a light which even staunch supporters of his struggle for Irish independence found unpalatable. In effect, it proved more damning for him to engage in acts of consensual lovemaking with others of his own gender than for him to consort with the German enemy of Britain, and Belgium's and Britain's decimation and extermination of tribal people on two continents under colonial oppression, for those nations to rob the natural wealth of the earth's wretched for squalid financial enrichment without cognizance of or conscience to any sort of morality.

So the brilliant lad of Sandycove, Dublin, who served as Conrad's mentor and guide in penetrating the horrors rampant in the Congo, swung, as the expression was, at Pentonville Prison in London, 3 August 1916, age fifty-one. Among the few who sustained their protest against this barbarity were George Bernard Shaw and Sir Arthur Conan Doyle. Joseph Conrad, on the other hand, turned his back on Casement in his hour of extremity. A true British stalwart, born in Poland, who had acquired English as his third language.

I've digressed from the plight of myself and Weymouth Smith, though I think not without justification. For the wickedness of yesteryear today has become miniaturized by such widespread, brazen flaunting of depraved indifference to all life, and with so much more than was at stake for the world in 1916, that the reader must need be reminded that jackals and freebooters and pirates roam the land freely, feast on the suffering of the poor with proud relish rather than make any attempt at concealment, and it is this, if anything, which occasionally half-persuaded me that Fu Manchu's schemes for world rule might not be half as malignant as those of our indigenous politicians and corporate magi, who are indistinguishable, and circulate between boardroom to government office and back again like rattlesnakes coiled about the hand grips of revolving doors.

But back to the dungeon. I'm a crack shot with a rifle, but had serious doubts about my skills with a blowgun the size of a cigarette holder, which Lilah had thoughtfully placed between my lips, loaded with a loop needle, hoping against hope that our next visitor would be anything other than Dr. Fu Manchu, and reminding myself not to inhale. Whilst we waited, Smith unusually silent and, for once, entirely reliant upon my own effort, I wondered what effect looping oneself would have. Would I erase my memory synapses and replace them with the same synapses, differently configured? Could one do a walk-in on one's own consciousness? Become a total blank?

The premonitory rustling far off in the outer hall had ceased, and total silence had enveloped us: and in that silence, I became convinced that I heard singing, a divine voice accompanied by the merest suggestion of stringed instruments. Not Lilah's voice, nor that of any woman I knew, yet the song it issued was suffused with an unearthly grace and a most earthy trace of long memory, trilling yet not gay-hearted, neither regretful nor joyous, but grounded in the singer's awareness that her vocal instrument was rendering a performance, tinged with indifference towards the hearer. I knew it had certainly to be an auditory hallucination, yet in that dank nowhere it suffused me with a feeling that life, whatever it held in store, whatever it had already inflicted, was simply life, take it or leave it.

You came along from out of nowhere/ You took my heart and found it free/ wonderful dreams, wonderful schemes from nowhere/ made every hour/ sweet as a flower to me!/ If you should go/ back to your nowhere/ leaving me with a memory/ I'll always wait for your return from your nowhere/ hoping you'll bring your love to me!

Of course, suffering stinks. I'd have given anything for the drab, ugly security of Land's End just then, though I also had begun to wonder what life there would be without the ectoplasmic Lilah. Had I, somehow, fallen in love at first sight of this angelic being? After the mess I'd endured with my ex-spouse, I had long ceased to entertain any amorous fantasies or wishes for another love. But now…

18

Now the unthinkable was occurring at Land's End: the somnolent population, normally invisible until nightfall, was appearing in ever greater numbers during the daylight hours: dazed, practically insentient but mobile enough to perambulate the streets, never acknowledging each other, or those of us who were not stricken with the strange narcoleptic malady.

The term *zombie* entered my thoughts more than once, but the ambulatory nocturnals exhibited no aggressive interest in others, but rather simply ambled slowly about, rudderless, sometimes stumbling over fixed objects such as fire hydrants or colliding with shop windows, most of which were clad in metal aprons, regaining wobblesome equilibrium with evident effort. They did not form any sort of pack, or divide into gangs, even those whom, at night, loudly greeted each other and boozed and whored in groups.

Life is strange, they say. Living death is stranger still. We began noticing, besides these semi-comatose wanderers, swarms of unfamiliar insects in the upper air, about the treetops, resembling winged mantises, with unusual feelers extruding from their heads, and discernible humps at the rear of their thoraxes: they seemed to manifest only during daylight hours, before our local bats made their nightly sweep of bugs whirling under the poorly wired streetlamps.

While maintaining my diurnal routine of opening Petrie's premises to Colecrupper, Thalidomido, Wellbutrin, and other of our flotsam and jetsam when these aggravating hangers-on materialized, I insisted that they keep their visits brief, their drainage of Petrie's remaining liquor supply to a minimum, and insisted that I was unwell, possibly with a contagious malady, which sent them scurrying at twilight time to the Scroop of Masham, where the otiose Sauerbrotten jubilated at their enhanced expenditure in his premises. Colecrupper favored the pub proper, where he sometimes ineptly attempted to score at dart-throwing and billiards, while Thalidomido, Wellbutrin, and the substitute coroner, Crashnitz, a kind of Petrie surrogate figure, favored the so-called beer and wine garden, where they had struck up some sort of amity with a garishly disreputable-looking pair of brothers: one, nearly moribund, named Morton, the other perhaps a decade younger named Bernard, who often brought along his fortyish son, a man with the features of a wolverine and, like his father and uncle, said to own at least a hundred of the most criminally neglected and rat-infested slum tenements in the unfortunate area of Land's End known as Kyklerville.

This family, the Treebarks, had established their enterprise of gouging the poorest of the Land's End destitute many decades earlier, and were figures of local notoriety, though until recently almost never seen, as they resided, I had heard, in suburban Quiffbush, an unincorporated region of northern Pyle. Both Treebarks were getting on – Morton recalcitrantly crawling graveward, so the locals gossiped, with accelerating loss of brain matter, and the delusional intention of taking the millions he'd pirated from his share of their jointly owned, half-collapsed slum structures into the Cemetery Beyond the Pale adjacent to the University of Pyle. The younger Bernard, notable mainly for a physical anomaly – a double row of rather sharp though seriously decayed teeth in his lower jaw – had earned a wide reputation for ruthlessness unseen since the twelfth century; a loathing son, Isnatch, had inherited this loathing like a genetic deformity, along with the double set of teeth. Isnatch was an especially unfetching piece of work, short and withered-looking like his relatives, with his father's feral eyes that sparkled with avarice, and a flatulent personality which, like Sauerbrotten's, packed plenty of Schadenfreude and amorality.

The Treebarks were, naturally, both loathed by Sauerbrotten, a voluble anti-semite (believing the Treebarks to be Jews, when in fact they originated in a subproletarian Cossack suzeranity of Uzbekistan) along with his other repulsive traits, for their imagined ethnic background, and cherished them as recent "regulars," for although they eschewed the groaning hog platter that was Sauerbrotten's speciality *de le jardin*, they consumed vast quantities of chicken innards, deep-fried chicken skin, and Sauerbrotten's beety but tasteless version of borscht, one of the menu's more obscure alternatives, and quaffed considerable pitchers of a disgustingly sweet wine Sauerbrotten had had festering in his cellars for years without managing to peddle a drop of it. Isnatch sometimes brought with him a slatternly cooze named Myriad Fingeryd, a "manager" for a realty firm that fronted for the Treebarks, Croupcough Circle Realty, notorious for bribing municipal building inspectors, certain brigades of the Land's End fire department, and Tesla Coil Electric Company officials.

The Treebarks had, once upon a time, emptied buildings they wished to demolish or "renovate," as they called their practice of slapping cheesily modern-looking improvements over "units" in perilously wired and decrepit structures, by filling vacant floors and apartments in these deathtrap architectural relics with desperate junkies, thugs recently released from prison, and former concentration camp guards, mainly from Poland and Ukraine. Alternatively, when it suited their needs, professional arsonists were engaged to artfully spread accelerant throughout the structures and gleefully set them ablaze.

Croupcough Circle, however, employed more subtle though

hardly less effective methods for optimizing profits for the Treebarks in parts of Kyklerville thickly inhabited by artists, who attracted the establishment of storefront galleries, which then displaced small businesses such as dry-cleaning establishments, tailor shops, neighborhood groceries, and the like, which, in turn, attracted bohemian sons and daughters of the well-to-do, who opened expensive boutiques and posh restaurants. These subsequently gave way to big-time real estate operators who, building by building, demolished whole neighborhoods in the area to erect monstrously tall, vastly expensive condominium apartment buildings of fantastic ugliness and chain outlets of drugstores and department store emporiums, attracting fresh branches of banks and so-called "superstores" indistinguishable from the corporatized hideousness of many areas of outer London and Glasgow. The transformation of Kyklerville, originally named for the Earl of Kykle, had built slowly from modest upgrade to a rapid, even disorientingly rapid turnover in rental locations that served as money laundries for Asian capital: Petrie, by the way, had remarked years earlier that "those planes aren't leaving the hangars." The most remarkable feature of the monoliths springing up from what had once been economically and ethnically mixed neighborhoods was that they were largely vacant and their "luxury units" served as *pieds-à-terre* for billionaires from Singapore and Malaysia.

Digitized capital flowed through these new jerry-built erections, all of it invisible, numerical, what used to be called "virtual," meaning "virtually nothing," a shell game played on small fluctuations of stock prices and rapid flow of money based on no tangible productive goods. Money that "floated free" of any moorings in the reality of products or services. What Charles F. Adams wrote in 1871 remained true in the present day: "The vast majority of stock operations are pure gambling transactions. One man agrees to deliver, at some future time, property which he has not got, to another man who does not care to own it."

While much of Land's End proper remained the derelict port and superannuated shipbuilding wreckage it essentially was, the future ruins of Kyklerville's homogenized, bleakly uniform lack of individual character was literally written all over its street-level walls in spraypainted runes and ciphers: always an omen of immanent desuetude and decline. The area's streets appeared chockfull of affluent persons, chattering busily into their iMe's or performing other brain-deadening operations on them (once called "multi-tasking," now known as "brain-waiving," scientifically proven to optimize inefficiency and deliquescence, while the "brain-waivers" exulted in the delusion that they were doing many things superbly well at the same time), but this, too, signified nothing more than a sort of frenzied stasis before the oncoming catastrophe.

If I have elaborated the pathologies of the Treebark Family, the Croupcough Circle Realty Company, and their affiliates at such length, it's merely to indicate the degree to which the ChoFatDong, captained by Fu Manchu, had advanced what we later learned to have been the Land's End Long Range Study into implementation long before the arrival of the Hybridized Insect Invasion and the arrival in Britain of the Cold Children.

Meanwhile, every evening, I made with Marco, and sometimes without Marco, a circuitous route to Khartovski's hovel, where Vanessa's presence had dispelled a goodly part of its customary glum. Still no signals from Petrie, but Vanessa adroitly synthesized the information now pouring in from Land's End and its surrounding region.

She had, for example, deduced that the influxing insects were genetic hybrids equipped with non-insect transmitters, akin to GPS devices, and that the garish homicides were gratuitous acts designed to distract the population from a far-reaching threat with many connecting ganglia. She unequivocally believed this the work of the ChoFatDong, speculating that its overall purpose was the conquest of the British Isles and subjugation of its inhabitants. Marco's skepticism quickly evaporated under the momentum of Vanessa's logical inferences.

For the moment, we could not devise a plan of counteroffensive, since certain matters remained unaccountable and impossible to suture together. Still, her reasoning was formidable.

"The question, as always, is what happens next. Might these cicadas, let's call them, also be armed with some kind of neurotoxin or other chemical weapon? And, what other weaponry has the ChoFatDong at its disposal?"

"Given what we're dealing with," Marco ventured, "it seems it could be anything, including things we can't imagine."

"The ChoFatDong specializes in things other people can't imagine. Remember, they operate according to no moral law and thus no inhibitions, imagination-wise."

Vanessa pondered. Khartovski wore a pensive expression as well, as though he were searching his mind for the missing fragment of a jigsaw puzzle. But it was Marco who spoke up.

"In Burkina Faso," he mused, "when a faction planned an attack, they used a three-prong approach: a terror campaign, like these killings, augmented by radio broadcasts to set one tribe warring with another. Then, an exact mapping of their enemy's resources and the location of their defensive positions. This would be followed by a sort of crude attack, using the least of its resources, as a feint for the real attack, which relied on an element of surprise. It was, usually, a surprise facilitated by infiltration."

"Excellent," Vanessa told him. "Let's surmise that Britain is being infiltrated. That the groundwork has been laid, that we can anticipate a preliminary, seemingly manageable assault, followed by whatever actions the infiltrators subsequently instigate."

Kartovski now spoke.

"We need to identify the infiltrators."

19

The next through the door of our keep, unfortunately, was indeed Dr. Fu Manchu himself. In his richly embroidered robe, his indelible green eyes, and, on his shoulder, clinging to his neck, a silvery-white creature with a prognathous lower face beginning at the nose, furled wood-mushroom-yellow ears, and four furry armlike legs equipped with sharp claws.

"So, my friend, we once again meet in an antagonistic, and on your part, powerless situation. Surely, Smith, you must have known lo these many years, that things would finish up in this manner."

Smith raised his chin and angled his head.

"I have often anticipated such an outcome," he rasped. Fu leaned in closer.

I realized Smith was attempting to manipulate Fu into a posture at which I could expel the information loop needle in the blowgun into Fu's optical nerve.

I gathered breath up from my lungs. Smith cocked his head and looked at me, drawing Fu's gaze in my direction.

I aimed. I blew. The loop needle struck the marmoset. A lamentable bad result, caused by the beast's shifting position. Miraculously, the needle penetrated undetected by Fu Manchu. Loop needles evaporate upon contact.

Surreptitiously pressing the front screen of the iMe2 as

instructed by Lilah, I now found myself gradually inhabiting the brain of the marmoset while retaining sentience within my own body.

"The time is not yet," Fu sibilantly declared. "I have a proposition for you to consider, and will leave you and Dr. Petrie by yourselves for another hour to form a decision."

My weight rested on the bony shoulder of Fu's silk robe. My furry forearms clung to his neck. I waited for Fu's "proposition."

"Join forces with me, Smith. You shall have the golden chance to assist in restructuring all life on earth along more coherent lines than your race has concocted in its thousands of years of gross ineptitude and self-interest. Your agile mind will be put to infinitely more useful purpose than the glorified, licensed killing you do for Scotland Yard."

I expected Smith to spit out a balking refusal. On the contrary.

"I shall give it my consideration."

My claws raked lightly at Fu Manchu's ear.

"Oh Cutie. Not now. Well, perhaps a bit lower down."

I considered my chances of clawing out Dr. Fu Manchu's eyeballs. And considered that these were not, of course, his only senses. I instead continued shifting about on Fu's shoulder, my claws fingering the filigree embroidery of his robe. His scent was powerful, the perfume of opiates, a trace of bergamot, a slight whiff of calamine lotion. I whimpered a bit, in an affectionate manner. Fu's fingernail carressed the furry crown of my head between the ears. His actual fingertips stroked the oval of my upper left ear.

"Treat for Cutie time," crooned the maniacal genius, returning my light scratch.

We repaired from the chilly cell, Fu locking the door behind us. I remembered the yellow button.

"Smith," I said from my shackled position, "prepare yourself to witness an astounding transformation of my physical being."

"I look forward to it," Smith shot back, with a soupçon of Smithlike japery.

I entered Dr. Fu Manchu's vast ovoid study on Fu's head, having scrambled up to a secure position on his geodesic skull with my hindquarters nestled in the roots of his pigtail. Fu moved deliberatively, floatingly for a cabinet from which he extracted a lacquered-inlaid box, carrying it to a wing chair of soft leather the color of Velveeta cheese. One broad arm of the chair supported the box. He flipped the lid, extracted a slender pipe roughly nine inches in length, slid open a compartment in the outer inlay, and from it extracted a ball of opium, which he packed into the gold bowl of his pipe.

Igniting the opium, he gently blew out the flame when it caught, drawing a lungful of narcotic. He held it an incredibly long time, then motioned for me to scramble down to his arm. I looked into his face with an adorably eager expression.

"Open wide, Cutie," the doctor gasped, withholding the smoke until I'd made a rictus into which he streamed a wavery tendril of the magic flute's special calmative.

After deep inhalation and the expected sensation of total peace, I vocalized several grunts or squawks of contentment. I no longer needed to cling to Fu Manchu. I could scramble, sloth-fashion, down the soft embroiderment of the chair, and torpidly wander the room.

I had never gotten so high in my life. I had never inhabited the mind of a marmoset in my life, either, and – a strange thing, this – found that I had a circuit channel to the brain in my Petrie body, and could mentally describe in fastidious detail everything my eyes and other senses came upon in Fu's… Shangri-La, I am tempted to call it, or at least, I was then.

"This is stupendous!"

Smith stared as my musculature diminished in thickness, my skull altered form, and I easily slipped my feet and hands free of the iron clamps.

"I'll say," Smith said. "You know something, Petrie, if I didn't know that was you, I'd mistake you for Buddy Holly."

I assumed this served as a compliment. With Smith one never could be sure.

"But what's also incredible, Smith, is that I can *see* what Fu Manchu is doing at this very moment!"

Not much, if truth be told, but nodding out, with visions of a Fu Planet waltzing through his mind like a Viennese operetta.

"Great Caesar's ghost, Petrie, can it be you took him over?"

How could I see what Fu was doing, if I were inside him? I would have to be gazing into a mirror, which Fu, I suppose, in a sense was, but his study contained no mirrors.

Which struck me as odd. Such a self-regarding rogue, you'd think, would look at himself all the time. But Fu, I believe, saw himself as the world, the world as himself, and, besides, so often assumed disguises that perhaps he had entirely forgotten what he really looked like. I have an aversion to mirrors, though as Cutie I'd have loved to preen myself before a looking-glass, provided I could recognize myself, rather than mistake my image for another marmoset.

"Not exactly, Smith. I seem to have taken over Cutie."

Taken over didn't quite describe it: a lot of Cutie remained in his simian mind, the scratching, the baring of teeth, the yearning to groom other marmosets, the glottal noises and incontinence.

"Huh. Still, we've got eyes on the avatar of evil, or you do. If I weren't in these damned restraints – "

But ya are, Blanche, ya are, came the old Bette Davis line unbidden.

A deductive leap performed itself while I scrambled along the carpet of Fu's *sanctum sanctorum.* An Isfahan carpet of spectacular Islamic design, like everything of Fu's in resplendant taste, but for the color of his chair. He even owned a Picasso from the Pink Period, and a Max Ernst of considerable renown. Like Sir Lionel Parker, Fu too had a globe of the earth in a carved wooden cuplike plinth, though Fu's featured the areas he imagined conquering in a violet color.

"I'll bet anything this iMe2 can perform a similar action on yourself, Smith: Lilah did say it was counterintuitive, and I'd hate to make some gross mistake. But – "

I studied the thing, which looked like a modified Blackberry, but I've never been adept with that sort of technology. Call me old-fashioned, the gewgaws of the modern world left me cold.

"Well, let me have a gander. I'm no Fu, but I'd wager I can figure it out. You keep an eye on our nemesis."

I crossed the room, adjusting to the gait of my modified organism, placing the iMe2 into Smith's hand, screenside outward. He mused silently. Technology wasn't Smith's strongest suit, either, though he'd scarcely admit it.

An East Indian whom Fu referred to as Ken Jay entered the oval office, two ash-grey Nubian bodyguards flanking him.

"I take it," said Fu, languidly, slouching into a menacing posture, "our wingèd accomplices are transmitting our survey data, are they not?"

"You are, as always, correct, Mein Herren."

Fu Manchu regarded Ken Jay as one might a lump of gristle in a stew. Such a craven, fat-assed geek. How could such a gargoyle produce a Lilah from his fatty loins?

"Herren? What sort of moronic appellation is that? A grovelling one, I presume. What are we picking up thus far from our bugs?"

Ken Jay unconsciously scratched himself on the arms. A lot of buggery seemed to be going around.

"Aerial videos of the entire eastern coast of England. A few have experimentally released their neurotoxins at low altitude."

I snarled, baring my fangs. Might as well throw the fear of Cutie in him. Ken Jay eyed me warily.

"Ah. Splendid. Move another squadron in to record the effects."

Dr. Fu Manchu could barely suppress a sallow gloat. Such fear and trembling over a wee tiny animal!

"Your command is my command, I shall do so instantly."

Ken Jay bowed and nearly fell on his face as he prepared his exit. The grey Nubians gave Fu a kind of Masonic salute.

"Oh, and Ken Jay," Fu added, insinuative, "after that mission's accomplished, you have my consent to briefly see Lilah."

Ken Jay's gratitude was appropriately excessive. From my vantage point high on a bookshelf, the man looked exhausted. Yet I scented cunning on his perspiration, an anticipation in excess of what might be released at the prospect of a conjugal visit with his daughter. Apparently, some of my senses were more acute than Fu Manchu's, for the doctor simply clasped his talon-like fingers and stared into space.

"Cutie, I'm growing sick of that grovelling schmuck."

I brayed in agreement.

"I'm really not sure about this," Smith told me. "I am… roughly familiar with the first generation iMe, but these programs – I really need to go into the system."

Smith knew the *lingua technica* but I knew he was stumped as a leper.

"Can't you simply reduce your size, as I did?"

I was catching a bit of Fu's gloating tone. Smith, prevaricating and bullshitting for a change, already seemed reduced in size, from my perspective.

"You forget, Petrie, that Lilah programmed this device for yourself. I need to change the password in order to access the morphing software."

As Smith hesitantly coded into the digital matrix underlying the decorative screen of the iMe2, I reported the titles of all the books on Fu Manchu's many shelves, keeping close watch on the doctor at the same time.

He had lifted the handset of an old-fashioned Princess

telephone and tapped in a number with an opalescent fingernail. He then placed the handset on a device which activated a conference call speak-easy.

"Klebb," came a gutteral female voice. It was either the connection, rather clearer in Paraguay than in Britain or the US, or else the speaker's vocal cords had been ravaged by cigarettes and whiskey.

"Roswitha, my Hummers will be delivering the Cold Children later this evening. They're having their naps, which they certainly need after their final hours of indoctrination this morning."

A pause followed. I knew nothing of Klebb, but she sounded less than ebullient.

"May I ask how many?"

Indeed, resignation gave her voice a heaviness that spoke of overwork.

"Twenty-five. That's all the Cold Children we'll need. The others I shall keep in storage until success is mine. Then they'll be incinerated. As it happens, I've got to keep Ken Jay and his precious ice queen alive while we're monitoring the launch of Phase Three."

The speaker crackled, Klebb worked up some animation.

"Guess what. The jeweler found seventeen zircons and four rhinestones mixed in with those diamonds."

A trace of I-told-you-so there. She held back some news, it sounded like.

"Bastards. I hope you had them killed."

A lurid chuckle. Or cackle.

"Better than that, I had the isotopes hijacked after handing them over."

Fu Manchu's face creased in displeasure. Not a guy who liked surprises, I gathered.

"I thought you were waiting on the appraisal."

Another pause, this one a quick-witted excuse.

"I was, Fu, but they seemed in such a godawful hurry – "

She would've run on, but Fu made a wave of impatience she

must have viewed in her mind's eye.

"Oh, like they're going to construct an atomic weapon with that crap we sold them."

He laid down his pipe, rose to his full stature, and wrathfully tapped out his irritation with the tips of his fingernails, aubergine on that particular day, on the surface of his Fu World Order globe before setting it aspin.

"They've been praying frantically down at the Sizzler. Naturally getting no response."

Fu laughed for the first time all day. He imagined preying on members of a twelve-step program called Terrorists Anonymous, that would go heavy on the "higher power" crap.

"Can't trace the hijack to you, I hope?"

All we need, bunch of Muslim imbeciles taking out one of my best agents.

"I may be fat and club-footed, my friend, but I'm no dumbbell."

So. Even with the zircons and rhinestones she collected plenty of the swag, and they could peddle the same crap to the Tamils in Sri Lanka.

"That you aren't. In fact, I sometimes call you that in conversation with my other intimates."

"Call me what, Clubfoot Annie? I knew it."

"No, dumbbell, *Not Stupid. Not Stupid del Este*, to be precise. Anyway, keep a low profile until we get you out of del Este."

Those Cold Children: perfectly trained and indoctrinated. Telepaths every one, and entirely bent to the will of Fu. Adopted into key British homes, the brats might not exactly set the world on fire, but they'd light up some lethal flames in quite a few hearts.

"I hope 'Más feo que el Pecado' comes to something like a season conclusion before I skedaddle."

"Fear nothing, my pet. I'm taping the episodes for you after you depart."

"I'm just curious as to – "

"How Claudia sabotages her treacherous friend, I'd wager."

"Telepathic as always, Master of the Universe. I've got my guesses, but that's one telenova always full of surprises."

"They will need to get shots to travel. The Cold Ones. But not from a vet. You'll administer them yourself. The requisite serums and so forth will be delivered, along with expertly forged entry visas, passports, and so on."

"You think of everything."

Everything except me, thinks Klebb. I'm nothing but a tool, like a lug wrench, to him.

"I do what I can, Klebb."

Yeah, yeah, yeah, Klebb thought. She'd heard this bogus holiday-type modesty from him before, usually when he planned sticking her in scalding hot water with Johnny Law.

Recounting every word to Smith, he prepared to switch the password of the iMe2. It came with a plastic pointer thing he worked with his teeth.

"Fucking thing wants more personal info than Inland Revenue," Smith grumbled. "Oh, I see. I hit 'Register in 14 days.'"

"No, Smith, hit 'Never Register.'"

Otherwise, I thought, it watches you while you watch it. Leaving cookies. Caches. Traceable items of all sorts.

"I'm in!" Smith exulted, for he really could be a technical klutz.

"Bravo, Smith." I couldn't resist sharing his triumphant mood. "Our opponent is no match for you."

Oh stop building him up, I reminded myself. Go all obsequious and he'll get careless.

"I wouldn't go that far, as a regular thing, but in this instance, Petrie, I think you're right."

At the risk of sounding like Smith, do not ask me what he did after gaining access to the iMe2 that produced the result that it did when he manipulated the touch screen. I can only tell you that, on the positive side, Smith became freed of his bondage.

On the negative side, painful as it is to relate, Smith's body not only shed its usual sturdy build, but became… miniaturized. I don't mean in the sense of a dwarf or a midget, but tiny, less than a foot in height. The iMe2 slid from his grasp, of course, and I caught it, fortuitously, before it struck the stone floor of our dungeon.

He now stood, fully erect, in the seat of the iron chair, issuing a stream of obscenities which his voice was too lacking in volume for me to decipher. Somehow his clothing had likewise diminished in size, and he looked exactly like himself as viewed through the wrong end of binoculars. Gesturing frantically, pointing his arm at the iMe2 device, I gathered he wanted me to discover a way to return him to his normal size.

My poor powers of concentration were such that I could not attend to Smith while the streaming telepathic information I received from my marmoset other self perceived the activities in Fu Manchu's office. I had scrambled down from the bookcases and now perched on Fu's massive desk, flapping papers about and transmitting whatever I could glean from them to myself.

If only Lilah would reappear! Surely she could put matters right with a few keystrokes. With this in mind, I went leaping for the door of Fu's command post and made adorable efforts to turn its brass knob.

"Cutie wants to roam about," Fu informed his phone mate. "Safe enough in this place, I suppose, though I perish at the idea of him getting confused in this labyrinthine house and finding his way outside in a panic."

I made burring noises of intense frustration, leapt up and down, and demonstrated such an immensity of feral anger I feared I might be confined to my cage.

"He won't get lost in that place," came Klebb's caustic voice. "It's sealed up tighter than a monkey's asshole."

My sphincter muscles contracted instantly. What a cunt, I

concluded. On the other hand, she was working in my favor.

"Very witty, Klebb. I suppose you're correct. Still, the cage might be a better place for him, what with all the comings and goings on this day of days."

End of days, more like it. The invasion of England had already commenced, and here I was, trapped in the body of a marmoset, Smith reduced to peanut size, my other body uselessly trapped with him in –

"For god's sake let him out. Even marmosets need a change of air."

Klebb, like Fu, had an opinion on everything.

"But the poor devil's stoned out of his gourd."

He had it there: I wondered if I could find the door, even as I was scratching at it.

"Thanks to whom?" Klebb snarled. "Probably needs to work off some of the high you've got him on."

To my amazement, Fu crossed the oval office and set the door ajar.

"Now, Cutie, don't meander about in unfamiliar territory. There are things in this house Papa Fu wouldn't want you to see."

"These damned electronic gadgets," I exclaimed to Tiny Smith, who had perilously leapt from the chair and was currently yanking at my trouser leg in irritation. "At least I'm at liberty to roam the corridors and open rooms, so shall probably find Lilah and manage to distract her guards long enough for her to return here."

I then recalled that Lilah had spoken of an escape scheme involving only herself and her father. Had they already fled?

I pranced as innocuously as possible through one of the strangest interiors I had ever beheld. There was a house within the house, circular in design, with a corridor like a race track tiled in Carrara marble. High above, circular chandeliers hung pendant from domelike skylights.

Smith paced our prison on his teensy shoes, restive as a shark tracking a pilot whale. I couldn't make out a word he said. He sounded like a noisy bug, sometimes like an entire swarm of cicadas.

"I feel certain that Lilah wouldn't leave this compound without saying goodbye."

I didn't comprehend Smith's buzzing reply.

"Oh, I'm so computer illiterate. I could kick myself, but I might hit Cutie by mistake."

The screen face of the iMe2, festooned with colored press-keys, screen savers, and advertisements of various kinds, at last yielded a legible sort of animated keyboard. On it, crude cartoonish icons were shown performing various prodigies of metamorphosis: a pudgy little elf shot up in height and shed its pot belly, a tearful greeting card manga-type wiped its eyes and offered a giggling grin, and so on. Just looking at this shit could drive a person mad, I thought, scanning for a miniature Hummel figurine or whatever that increased its proportions and shot up in height.

One wall of the antechamber of the inner structure had even-ly spaced, massive arched windows of wrought iron, shaped into patterns suggestive of Islamic carpets, curlicues, and spokelike extrusions from circular insignia. Curiously, both the swastika and the Star of David were represented in these circles, attesting to their origin before the former became the symbol of Nazism, as did their design, which had been modified from the Aryan swastika that once decorated first editions of Rudyard Kipling's tales and novels. Masonic images and heraldry also appeared along the interminable circular corridor.

Against the opposite wall, a series of doors: not any old doors, but elaborately fashioned portals of teak carved in Hindu reliefs. Where in the name of anything was I? I loped along, monkey that I partially was, in search of Lilah's chambers. Smith kicked a cockroach that seemed interested in him across the dungeon.

I felt free as a marmoset and imprisoned like a convict. The sight of Smith all tiny like that distressed me. I didn't trust my counterintuition enough to fool around. I needed to see that icon that would restore him to normal size. Moreover, he would be the one who would have to tap it. At least he wasn't getting any smaller. In my faraway youth, I saw a film, *The Incredible Shrinking Man*, in which a man on a boat passed through some malignant mist and began shrinking, shrinking, ever shrinking, until he became "the infinitely small."

I suppose we are all the infinitely small when you get right down to it. Smith had always been infinitely large in his own head, and no doubt Dr. Fu Manchu, in his, was the size of the known universe. But when push comes to shove, we're all just pieces of lint and, hey, what's the difference? What I can't stand is pain, the pain I did not so much feel as considered I felt as I shook my rear end as monkeys do, in search of Lilah. Shook, that is to say, up and down, rather than side to side.

"This has to be it," I told myself, loping over to a teak double door, telling myself, at the same time, that it most certainly wasn't it: I pressed my curled little ear to the wood, and with arduous concentration could make out voices. The voices – could it really be? – of Ken Jay and Lilah!

"Father, really, not here. Not now."

I heard struggling sounds, the obscene panting of Ken Jay, some fabric ripping within.

"Lilah, it is months since release of my seminal fluids! I need this jism squirt to keep my mind clear of distracting thoughts."

Talk about feeding a girl a line of hooey. He thinks he's Sterling Hayden in *Dr. Strangelove*. I had nothing against incest *per se*, half of Land's End had resulted from it, but when it came to the woman I adored –

"You're a pig, father, sorry to say so. Besides, we must think of freeing Obregon and Inspector Smith."

She called me Obregon! Could it be true? That Lilah, that

sublime creature, could… *love me?*

"But we only have a short time to make our way to the tunnel," Ken Jay protested.

"All the more reason for you to get your stubby mitts out of my sarong, father. And think about how to rescue them."

Resolve and rage percolated in Lilah's voice.

"We must leave them to their fate, Lilah."

And what if things were the other way around? Would Ken Jay like being left to his fate? With a perv like him, you never knew.

"Said like a true cringing coward," Lilah told him scornfully. "Which is why I refuse to go into the tunnel without Obregon at my side… or behind me, depending on the tunnel's width."

Ken Jay tried didacticism. Oh, if only I could be a fly on that wall! Well, not a fly, perhaps.

"It's not really a tunnel, Lilah, it's more like a portal. We still don't know where we'll emerge when we enter it."

Lilah's disgust dripped all over him.

"Perhaps an alternative universe. Who the fuck cares, Dad, as long as we get out of this one. But first things first."

Marching footsteps. I monkeyed my way up to the space between one of the wrought iron window embellishments and the inner wall of the outer house: those windows looked out upon a solid expanse of pink sheetrock. But I huddled in one corner as a sort of honor guard of tall ashen Nubians strode heavily armed along the curved corridor, followed by… children. Children of roughly eight and nine years of age, their ethnicities all mixed, some white, some yellow, some brown, and so forth, curiously identical in expression, though their faces varied considerably.

Just the sight of them gave me the horrors. They moved as a single unit, telepathing each one's perceptions, and they'd been dressed in really tacky school uniforms, like an army of North Korean think-alikes.

If any of these creepy kids glanced at the window they must have taken me for a dust mote, for they continued trekking behind the Nubians without a pause. When they had passed out of hearing and sight, I slipped through the wrought iron maze and scrambled to the doors behind which Lilah and Ken Jay continued their colloquy:

"Would you stop looking at those damned monitors and pay attention?"

"Such language, Lilah."

"At least I speak as I mean. All you do is grovel and grope and wring your hands helplessly. For christ's sake be a man for once, a real man. Not a cringing lackey or a drooling rapist. We've got to get Obregon and Smith out and then go to the portal."

Her words, I guess, cut him to the quick. It was about time.

"All right, already. Still got the duplicate keyring, I hope."

"I'm not an idiot like some I could name."

"All right. But don't blame me if we're caught in flagrante."

How much of her clothing had he ripped off? I vowed to make the obese bastard pay for his transgressions, and for holding everything up with his mad lusts.

"There's nothing to you worth blaming, as far as I'm concerned. You've used me like a Kleenex since I was eleven. No more, no more. I may be your daughter, as such I respect you, sort of – but let's cut the chatter and move."

Looking back, time left no other options. I picked the least grotesque of the icons and placed it on the floor where Smith could press it with his itty bitty finger. The result may not have been ideal, but it was better than turning him into a piglet.

20

"We stay awake all night," Vanessa remarked. "While the nocturnals roam around all day. Interesting field reversal phenomenon. I venture out in daylight – the fields and woods behind the row houses. I never run into them. In any case, they're harmless. Can't get it up while the sun shines, I gather."

They didn't stray outside the central village, as far as I'd observed. They haunted the places they'd always gone, but didn't see these places, or each other. Some gravitational force kept them anchored to the settings of their lives, like iron filaments clinging to a magnet.

"I wish I had a clue what was going on here," I said. My speech impediment, miraculously, had diminished to a mild stammer in the course of my nocturnal meetings with Vanessa and Khartovski. Marco wasn't present on this occasion: she'd asked me to tell him nothing about it.

"I've caught one of the bugs. With a butterfly net. I have it in a mesh box. I've been studying it all day."

Vanessa never wasted a minute. She had a definite objective in mind. Everything she did, she went at with maniacal concentration. It was as if she had occupied Zryd's orchestra as a pretext or a disguise, and known all along she'd end up here, at Khartovski's.

"Hope you had surgical gloves on."

I pictured her prodding a randomly captured specimen from the swarms that had arrived from nowhere. I realized then what was strange about her: nothing surprised her. She accepted everything as plain fact, folded events into her calculus without any sense of calamity. For her, the uncanny was natural and nothing to write home about.

"Gloves and a beekeeper's bonnet. Could've done with a gas mask, too. I've been probing it with acupuncture needles."

"What is it?"

"A genetic freak. Generations of them have evolved in a lab. How many generations in how short a time, I can't tell."

She motioned me to the cage. Inside, a hybrid two-and-a-half inches long, ugly as they come. She'd snipped off one of its antennae, which lay on the wheeled metal table where the cage rested.

"A transmitter. Here – " a cursory tap with a needle. "This raspberry hump behind the thorax. I think it contains a toxin. I don't want to puncture it."

It resembled a mantis crossed with a grasshopper, extruding bladelike, iridescent green wings from something else. Vanessa had evidently sedated it. Its movements were lugubrious and tentative, its single feeler drooping.

"I'm pretty good with electronics. So's Khartovski. Trouble with this bugger is, we really need a chemist to detach that lump and determine what's in it. Bats or birds that eat these may die. They learn a lot faster than we do what to avoid eating. So, it has no natural predators. Tell me something. Do you know the coroner filling in for Petrie? That Crashnitz in Puketown or wherever? Coroners often have chemical tracer equipment. Question is, can we trust him."

"I don't know him. From the looks of him, no."

Vanessa nodded. She gave the insect another poke.

"Yeah, I figured. If that Mavis companion is a nurse I'm Marie of Romania. Still, there's here's got to be a way…"

Khartovski lit a few candles under the icons, then poured himself a glass of kvass. The floor creaked under his feet. Roaches scuttled in the wainscotting.

"Wait. I have an idea. We capture another one, put them together in the cage. Then puncture one of the toxin sacs, see what happens. Or – we've got plenty of mice scampering around. I'm not a big fan of animal experiments but let's face it – "

"Better a rat than a mouse," Khartovski piped up. "Basement's surging with them."

His eyes shone.

"I like mice," he whispered, as if they could hear him. "I hate rats."

A rat or two, here or there, wouldn't overturn the world's ecological balance, or what remained of it. Mice and rats, sparrows and hawks. Khartovski had definite views about animals. Some were darlings, some were devils.

"We'll need to make a leakproof environment. Plastic dropcloths. Something we can seal and still see what goes on."

Petrie had an empty tropical fish aquarium somewhere in his house. In the conservatory, I recalled. I placed it firmly in my mind. I wanted to get in and out of there, unseen, as fast as possible. Petrie had indulged a brief fascination with fish, but got confused about the water pH levels. A solid, leakproof lid on it might do the trick.

I followed a devious route to Petrie's. A terrible fear had washed over me.

This indirect path detoured around the hub of Land's End, at an elevation from which its sordid emporiums, empty of all except sailors and barmaids now, could be viewed at a safe distance.

Once I'd entered Petrie's house I moved through it in the dark. A light might bring our usual menagerie, or worse. I couldn't account for my terror, but overturned the fake Tiffany lamp as I groped for the aquarium. It rested near Petrie's pipe stand, just as I'd envisioned.

The bizarre objects in the curio cabinets. Forlorn in the darkness, preserved but forgotten.

I knew I would not be returning. I knew once I slipped out and took my alternative circuit to Khartovski's, I'd not see Petrie nor Land's End for a long time. (When I did return, as a visitor, a year later, he'd leased out my rooms to a new tenant. By then we were all different people, unglued from the flypaper of the accursed town. That's a story for another time, however.)

To reach Khartovski's, I followed a sunken, abandoned rail track that ran down a sloped netherland beneath the ramparts of Gin Lane and its surroundings. A forgotten outskirt of weeds and thistles.

I knew a passage through a disintegrating glass-blowing works, in which shards of industry lay about in dusty heaps, a rust-belt warehouse structure now, where virtually no one ever appeared, least of all timorous me. But I had learned the route over many months. I felt strangely safe in these haunting byways. A tall, skinny youth, hugging an empty fish tank and moving through a labyrinth of oxidized I-beams and dusty flooring.

I passed through the past. A time when vast areas of towns truly were deserted, fallow, below the radar of developers and the teeming masses that followed them in their rape of all empty space.

While I moved through sites of future K-Marts and Walgreens and the other shit making its way from the country of the fat and stupid across the waves, Khartovski was busy cornering a rat in his basement, seizing the foul-snouted vermin with a set of fireplace tongs.

Vanessa continued her dissection of the snipped insect antenna, puzzling over its gel of microcircuitry.

I had had time to ponder why she didn't want Marco around. Perhaps she had fearsome visions about him, as I did. If not the satanic visions I conjured at Petrie's house, the little instinctive kind you hardly mention, even when you're paranoid. And who isn't?

She didn't glance up from her labors when I entered, hauling the glass container.

"Put that on this trolley," she said. Khartovski dropped the wriggling rat into the glass box and held it there as Vanessa lowered the mesh cage, plucking its lid open with an acupuncture needle.

The rat sniffed the insect, which stumbled repeatedly as it attempted to climb out. Khartovski clamped a thick baking pan over the open top. Then we sealed it with electrical tape.

"We might as well let the rodent eat the bug, see what occurs. We can always get more insects. Once I've got this antenna sussed out, we can alter them. Amputate and reattach them."

The damp rat warily eyed potential food. Then retreated to the opposite end of the aquarium.

"Neurotic type," Vanessa decided. We three gazed through the glass sides, waiting for something, anything: once, the insect spread open its wings, like a yawn, and folded them again.

"I hope one or the other makes up its pea brain."

"Their minds aren't exactly vast," Khartovski said. "Eat and shit, is about the size of it."

"Like people," sighed Vanessa. "Like billions of people we need like an army of rats."

She ceased crouching, stretched, and moved to the dining table. She yawned. I yawned.

"You'll miss the fun," Khartovski told us, still rapt with attention.

"What fun?" Vanessa yawned again, vigorously.

Khartovski now yawned too. He joined us at the table, several feet from the metal cart. He resisted a second yawn, but finally succumbed.

"Got any cards? We could play blackjack." Her elegant nonchalance belied all enthusiasm.

"I'll deal," I offered.

Khartovski slipped into his wreck of a bedroom, returning with an oily deck of ornate Russian playing cards.

I dealt Vanessa two cards, Khartovski the same, me the same, theirs face-up, mine one face-down.

"Hit me," said Vanessa.

Khartovski motioned for one card only. We now all yawned in unison.

"Stand." Vanessa had two nines.

"Shit." Khartovski stared hapless at a four and a six. *Rien à faire.*

The banker drew a hard eight.

"Fold," I said.

"Guess I take it."

There was nothing to take but the win.

Thirty hands later, the rat appeared to have fallen asleep. The bug crept near it on jointed legs, and ran its single antenna over a bit of its probably smelly fur.

"Oh, fucking do it, gas the little bastard." Vanessa didn't sound impatient, just bored.

"We're not betting," she declared. "We should bet something. How many minutes it will take, or which one eats the other."

"More like how many hours."

"Let's start with minutes, otherwise we'll only play one hand an hour. We'll all fall asleep."

"How about we bet on how long we have to keep playing."

Vanessa shook her mane of curls.

"We could switch to strip poker." Khartovski attempted a giggle. Like all horny Russians he thought he could jest his way into some action.

"I'm not showing my tits to you jokers."

Vanessa cupped her breasts protectively.

"My whang's nothing to write home about either."

Khartovski palmed his crotch in self-defense.

"I didn't say I was *flat*," she snipped. "Just not in a showy mood."

I stood up and ran my hands over my buttocks, like a ripe imbecile.

"I'm told I've got a nice firm ass," I said.

We were all uncomfortable with this unbuttoned infantility, but braving it out to keep ourselves conscious.

"Oh," said Vanessa. "Like I don't. Forget it."

"Gin?"

"I'd swallow some," she told me. "Hate the game, though."

"We're fresh out. Cleaning lady drinks it all."

"She certainly doesn't clean."

"Some Bacardi, though. A whole bottle."

"Dark or light?" Vanessa quizzed. "I can't stand dark rum. Reminds me of Surabaya."

We were weighing the pros and cons of craps or Old Maid and slurping mojitos when something moved in the tank.

The rat, who'd looked moribund, suddenly lunged and snapped off one of the insect's legs, chewing it with its nasty pincer teeth. Its red eyes glowed with rat glory. The mantislike bug cocked its triangular head, as if to say, "If that's all you've got, you're ratmeat."

It opened a valve in its raspberry lump.

We carried our drinks close to the enclosure. Whatever exuded from the bug's hump was colorless, and, naturally, we couldn't tell if it smelled like anything.

The rat convulsed. Flopped on its back, its bent legs twitching. Didn't look dead, though.

"Huh." Vanessa tapped a tooth with her fingernail.

"Now what," I said.

She shrugged.

"We wait." She scratched her coppery hair. "Shit, am I getting fleas in this place?"

It would have been surprising not to get fleas in Khartovski's place, cleaning woman or no cleaning woman. After all, we'd just dangled a rat around with the fireplace tongs.

"This is worse than reading Gladkov," Khartovski remarked.

Vanessa scrutinized me. I reminded myself that I was unusually comely, but hardly imagined that mattered to her.

"How's your night vision?"

I felt trapped in a horror movie. Rat, weird insect, three people in a Samuel Beckett hovel, plotting the capture of another insect.

"Pretty acute. Not acute enough, maybe, but I can try."

This would be the scene where yours truly would be devoured by the swarm, I imagined.

"They probably nestle in tree leaves. Hold the net under a branch and give it a good shake. You might get lucky."

I reflected that I'd never gotten lucky in my whole existence, but that was a side issue.

"You never know," Vanessa said.

I couldn't let that sit.

"Yes, you do."

She gave me what they call a "sidelong glance."

"Humor me. We'll just be grogging and keeping an eye on those two anyway."

Vanessa thought the invading insects, since night surveillance must have been part of their mission, could communicate with visual signals, like fireflies. She'd found at the apex of the captive's antenna a tiny bead of ultraviolet light. If this had been adapted from a firefly species common in Malaysia, these lights would, after a stuttering start, blip in syncopation, pulse off and on in the same instant, over vast areas.

How to describe the still-unruined woodland and intact meadows outside Land's End's aggregate of human filth? Quadrants of what Britain must once have been carried scents of pine, of wild grasses, pristine marsh and wildflowers. They rose from an earth soft and springy underfoot, the woods crackling as you stepped on dry leaves and pine needles, twigs and creeper ivy. If it took time for my eyes to adjust to the dark, soon the stars and a glorious half-moon revealed trees by its strong light. I then saw the flickering insect armies of the night, as Vanessa had predicted, spitting violet light off and on in harmony, an archipelago of invisible beings spread across meadows, across the forest, their presence assuring each other of their unbroken connection.

The peace of those wild expanses flushed away the town's desuetude, the must of Petrie's drawing room, the rancid butter stench of Khartovski's greasy lair: above, constellations and planets multiplied in a bowl of blue-black ether, an infinitude where shooting stars and comets soared across unimaginable, silent distances. Neither benevolent nor malign, beyond the reach of our interference. Even the satellite junk orbiting close to earth had joined a timeless order of "something taking its course" over billions of millennia.

I hadn't experienced such exhilaration in years. The woods cast a spell, as if I had entered a dream of something, something until that moment forever squashed and stultified. I had a magnificent sense of insignificance.

Strings of tiny violet lights expired and revived in micro-seconds. Soon I had entered a grove of new growth, with branches low enough for my high, skinny reach, and, net held open beneath, shook it "by surprise" until I heard one of the bugs drop inside, quickly bunched the netting with my fingers, and tramped back in the direction of Land's End. The meadows were damp with incipient dew, and soon the less natural light glowing within Khartovski's place confirmed that I had, actually, captured another… whatever it was. Indeed, not one, but three! Only then did their green wings and speckled abdomens appear: they didn't struggle at all in the net, but lay there like a catch of flopping fish.

"Bra-vo!" Khartovski exclaimed, eyeing the capture as I entered.

I had no idea how long or far I'd traversed the truly outer

world, but felt refreshed and ready for more absurd activity.

"No time flat," Vanessa answered my unasked question. "Now we've got a really adequate sample to study. Good work. Excellent. Oh, yeah, the rat woke up and ate the bug. We're waiting now to see if the rat explodes or something."

"At least I won't miss the climax."

21

In the matter of Weymouth Smith's enlargement by means of the iMe2, applying his half-inch palm to the icon I indicated after entering the password he'd reconfigured, I will readily admit, and sincerely regret, however amicably our later relationship was resolved, that I goofed.

In my own defense, I ask the reader to imagine the world he or she lives in as one immense, overcrowded, flat screen dizzying the eye and the mind with incessantly morphing images, of words changing into pictograms, pictograms shifting into numbers, crude representations of creatures and objects both extant and extinct, and choosing among this pandemonium of brightly colored, illusionary formations of pixels the rough approximation of oneself, or of one dear to your heart: and Weymouth Smith, for all his bluster and vainglory, was a man I deeply respected for his perspicacity, his devotion to his work, however bloody and ruthless it necessarily was, and, dare I say it even now, his friendship.

At the same time, the form he assumed after earnestly following my indication was not the Weymouth Smith as I had known him, or at least bore precious little visible resemblance to him. The same acute mind inhabited the mythological figure he assumed, which I have since identified as that of Agni, the god of fire, and messenger of the gods, a being with faces on opposite sides of its head, seven arms, and three legs, comely enough in his general aesthetic effect but virtually naked, but for chainlike bracelets around each wrist and necklaces of precious stones, a cluster of pendant jade earrings, and a headdress resembling a pagoda: each of his parts were perfectly formed, prehensile, and distinctly human, but even the thick moss of black hair extruding from the fringe of his headdress differed in color from Smith's oak-brown shag.

Facing in two directions at once, his perspective must not have been unlike my own mental life at that moment, my mind trapped in both my real body, or rather my altered but recognizable body, and that of Fu Manchu's marmoset, Cutie. Like myself, Smith initially experienced the confusion of being split, his attention circuiting between two different ways of looking at the world around him. Alas, both pairs of his eyes were seeing opposite views of the same skanky stone cell, while I, as Cutie, took in both the outside and the inside of our enclosure.

On the other hand, Smith quickly mastered the use of seven hands and arms, with one of which he made to slap me firmly across the face, but stopped himself, one face sinking into an expression of deep thought, the other avid in surmise at the possibilities offered by the multiplication of his dexterity. Fortunately, he had not lost the power of speech, though his manner of speaking had considerably changed.

"I shall not be thwarted in my mission," he announced in a tone appropriate to a cathedral pulpit, "to rid the world of Dr. Fu Manchu. Nor, Dr. Petrie, shall I pause in my quest to sort out the unbelievable fuck-up you have, no doubt unwittingly, foisted upon my corporeal form."

I meekly suggested that somehow summoning Lilah with the aid of my marmoset double might be the most expeditious way of correcting the error.

"I concur, but you must do your damnedest, lest you be damned to a lifetime of self-recrimination."

"Please, Smith, speak to me as a friend, not an opponent."

"For the time being, you will kindly address me as Agni, god of fire."

"Then Agni," I said, "do let's see what we can accomplish working in concert."

"Agni, god of fire, to you, defrocked physician. If your marmoset persona must claw its way to Lilah and immolate itself in the process, it is the will of Agni."

"Gee whiz," I exuded. "He's just a cute little innocent monkey."

"The cute and the ugly are equally ripe now for sacrifice," proclaimed Agni. Agni, god of fire, I might add.

This gave me an idea.

"If now you are the god of fire and messenger of the gods, perhaps you can unbolt our prison by means of incineration."

"Immolating you, to say nothing of myself?"

"No, I meant zapping the bolts on that steel door frame."

Yet Smith's, or Agni's, other face had a quite different personality, akin to Smith's own.

"My other half's just having at you, old man. I haven't changed an iota. Well, obviously I have, but only for the nonce."

A streak of coral and blue flame struck the door from one of Agni, god of fire's outstretched palms.

"Thus far, this Cutie you speak of has proven ineffective."

"Maybe he's succeeded in getting her attention," Agni/Smith's other half speculated.

And indeed, through my marmoset eyes, I already perceived the doors of Lilah's chambers opening, and figures emerging, her ineffectual father trailing the hem of her sarong like a meaching subject.

"Cutie!" she exclaimed, as I revealed my diminutive form and scrabbled up her richly patterned sleeve. "I must go now to Obregon. To Dr. Petrie. Can you understand what I'm telling you?"

I made vociferous noises of comprehension and eagerness. She held a heavy ring of keys, which I have already mentioned, and the Ken Jay creature followed cringingly behind her, nervous as a cat shitting razor blades.

"This is madness," he told her.

"I'll let you know what madness really is if you utter another fatuous remark, Father. Cutie, lead the way, if you can."

Not so simple. The circular building had the promise of danger at every curve.

We encountered the Nubians, but they knew only Lilah had Fu Manchu's utter trust, enough to expose her to Cutie without suffering a possibly infectious bite and a vicious clawing: they believed she'd been entrusted with delivering herself and Ken Jay to the Mandarin of diabolism's presence.

"I've grown fond of this place," Lilah sighed. "Not its myriad horrors, of course, but the architectural ingenuity that went into its construction. Too bad we can't have something of this type in Poona."

"But Lilah," Ken Jay meekly protested. "It would cost millions to construct."

"Fool," she reprimanded. "Not using Indian labor. Granted, the Taj Mahal cost a pretty penny. But that was the majestic *aide-mémoire* to a lost love. I intend to find my live one."

The Petrie in me tingled with emotion. In furry hops and ape-like haste, I guided Lilah and her terrified progenitor to the dungeon, which she hastily unlocked, having made a notch on the appropriate key.

"Smells like the thing is on fire," she said, worried. But the scorched door yawned open, and the sight of two-faced Agni, god of fire, seemed not to surprise her at all.

"What a klutz you are, darling Obregon. Gave Smith a bit of his own back, I see."

"Whom are thee?" Agni, god of fire, demanded to know.

"Lilah!" his other half exclaimed. "You see what fooling around with an iMe2 can cause."

"I do indeed. Drop the Agni, god of fire, crap, Smith, you're a bad poker player. Taunting dear Dr. Petrie with your *folie de grandeur*."

Instantly the Agni-half of Smith cackled merrily.

"And here I thought I'd pulled the wool."

"I'm sure you nearly gave him a heart attack. Now hand me that goddam thing before you turn yourself into a rhinoceros."

One of Smith's seven hands relinquished the iMe2, and Lilah instantly set to work, demanding his password, scrolling the screen with a button both Smith and myself had failed to notice.

"You'll be something like yourself in no time," she told him. "And then the four of us will make for the portal."

"Portal?"

"Tunnel, portal, dad's found something in the debris of the Masonic Temple round the bend from our suite. Where it leads I haven't a clue, and needless to say, this one – " she tapped Ken Jay rather forcefully on his pate, "has even less of an idea where it leads."

"But where's Fu? He's given us an hour for me to turn thumbs up or down on a lurid proposed amalgamation of forces."

"Fuck that. Fu's toast, if you want to know the truth. The ChoFatDong is about to be routed from Great Britain, appearances to the contrary."

22

Could Lilah somehow have known that Vanessa Savage had now thoroughly dissected those mandibled monstrosities and isolated the toxin their raspberry sacs carried?

The rat neither exploded, nor evidenced any other ill effects than the torpor of a satisfying meal.

"As I half-suspected," she said, "their poisons got diluted in transport. They didn't travel well. These GPD modules aren't so hot, either. Fu's probably getting a great aerial survey of Nova Zembla."

"What other menace might comprise the triangulated attack?"

"England's about to find out."

"Well, we've got to nip it in the – "

"Let England nip itself. Gentlemen, we're getting out of this land of hope and glory, courtesy of Singapore Airlines. First class. My mother's still good for something."

"We're England's only hope!" I said.

"Your Scotch, and Khartovski's Georgian. If England can't handle it, that's its problem."

Before you could say whiskey sour, or Miss Martini, a hired car pulled up in front of Khartovski's icky residence. We scrambled inside, and were speeding to Heathrow without so much as a fare-thee-well.

On the motorway, I stammered: "You said your mother was designing sets for Rautavaara's *Rasputin*."

"Oh, that too. But she faxes the designs."

"Well, where is she?"

"Use your imagination. Or don't, as you please. There is only one place *my* mother could possibly be, dontcha know."

Within two hours, we had boarded a flight for the Far East. Within another two hours, it cleared for departure.

I spread a small spoonful of Beluga on a lightly buttered toast point.

"Vanessa, you're incredible."

"And Sam – your name *is* Sam, ain't it? – Khartovski's not nearly as sick as he looks."

In fact Khartovski, at that moment, had his mouth stuffed with smoked salmon, washed down with Cristal.

"Boys, there's only one place on earth for the likes of us, and we'll be there in fourteen hours."

23

"I sabotaged the whole works," Ken Jay revealed. "There'll always be an England."

"Don't count on it," Lilah said as she wiped the icons from the iMe2 screen, revealing the Lexus code they concealed. "There's still the Cold Children en route there with Klebb. I take it," she told me, "you and Cutie here have… gotten to know each other. With your permission, Obregon, I'd like to keep you conjoined a bit longer. Send Cutie back to Fu's lair. We need some news."

Marmoset Me obediently scuttled from the dungeon Fu-wards.

In his oval office, Fu, glazed in the Velveeta wing chair, listened incredulously to a conference call while the four of us hurried to the Masonic Temple.

"Wretched," came Klebb's lounge singer's rasp. "We've been detained at Manchester Airport."

"On what grounds," Fu Manchu demanded.

"They found traces of heroin in my Louis Vuitton."

"Klebb, you imbecile!"

"It was your idea to store the stuff in my apartment."

"It wasn't my idea for you to start mainlining it."

"I told you. I was just chipping. Anyway, I keep my suitcases in that same storage room. Some of it must have sprinkled itself into an open bag. Have you vaporized Ciudad del Este?"

Fu now gave vent to a distinctly un-Fu-ish funk of depression.

"My appliance failed. Once again. The element I believed we'd found after decades of search... well, the thing works well enough on small objects. The OED, in the boxed set with the magnifying glass in the slide drawer, but it doesn't even vaporize a mosquito."

"I'll get the Cold Children through Customs, Fu, once this confusion's cleared up."

"Sorry, Madame," a clipped British voice broke through. "We need to quarantine these charges of yours. Six months at a minimum, and the time for your telephone call has expired."

"You've still got the kanaimà!" Klebb managed to shout before being cut off.

"Oh, ain't we got fun," Fu grumbled to himself.

"Time to disengage you from Cutie," said Lilah as we approached the area of the Masonic Temple where Ken Jay had found the portal. She snipped the effect of the loop, at the same time restoring Weymouth Smith to his normal self, if one could call him that.

Ken Jay slid aside a cheap plywood panel.

"It's dark," he said.

"It's narrow," observed Smith.

"In we go anyway," Lilah told us, pushing her father into the abyss.

Words cannot describe the sensations induced by entry into that portal. Well, they can. Vertigo, an acceleration of physical movement that felt likely to render my flesh to shards, and motion sickness you wouldn't believe.

Seconds later, I was expelled onto an expanse of green. Green baize, to be precise. A second after that, Smith landed on top of me.

"You didn't tell your mother you were bringing a pair of pooves with you," an intricately nuanced female voice said.

"They're a team, Mother."

"That I can see with my own eyes. You know these things are certainly allowed here, but not in my establishment."

"Not *that* kind of team."

"Of course not. A mere joke, Lilah. This is Inspector Weymouth Smith of Scotland Yard, from the country whose business concession nearly ran me out of the International Zone back in 1941. Beneath him your paramour, Obregon Petrie."

Smith rolled off my back and laid on his own, facing a woman of mystery whom I still had not seen.

"You can come up for air now, Dr. Petrie," said the mystery voice. "Welcome, gentlemen, to my humble house. I am Mother Gin-Sling."

I rolled onto my back. I saw above me a slender woman with the most elaborate and bizarre hairdo I had ever seen: a severe, imperious, impervious face, with a knowing smile that spoke volumes about how many times she'd been to the proverbial rodeo. She held her hands clasped in a curious way.

"Fortunately for our other guests this evening, no one seems interested in playing baccarat tonight. All the action is at the roulette table, and poker in the salon privé."

"I didn't mean to give you a nasty surprise, having father pop through the portal first," said Lilah.

"Viola, you know that Ken Jay is not your father. He has imagined a whole history of a life in Poona that he prefers to live in than the liquid reality we actually inhabit."

"I've encouraged him shamelessly. It seemed the best way to manipulate him."

"Obviously, you've done well. I suppose we all exist in one another's imaginations. And, I gathered, Fu has been incorrigibly harsh with him, no wonder he lives in a fantasy world."

I now piped in: "Lilah, how did you know where the portal led? You said your father – "

"He's not my father. I don't even know him."

"You said Ken Jay discovered the portal by chance."

"My name isn't Lilah, Obregon. I grew up right here, you see, and it was from here that we abducted Ken Jay. But we persuaded him, I did, I should say, that his actual daughter had been abducted with him."

"What is here?"

"This," said the mystery woman, "is a casino in Shanghai, open 24 hours."

Weymouth Smith appeared dazed and confused: a rare treat for yours truly.

"Right now," Mother Gin-Sling told us, "you are in what is known as no-space no-time. The architecture of this casino is highly malleable and so are your perceptions of it. I won't tell you more right now. But make yourselves at home in the future past."

24

Smooth as silk to Kuala Lumpur, read the plasma panel on the moving rubber sidewalk in Pudong International Airport in Shanghai.

The evenly spaced panels assured steady credit, smooth international financing of projects in Dubai, the eternal reliability of Rolex watches, the immutable security of family groupings, the preservation of their "memories" in the latest camera technology, and among many other things the absolute dependability of surveillance companies: "See and hear a pin drop in Lima from your work station in Bucharest," for example, illustrated by a generic male in impeccably handcrafted shoes crossed at the ankles near his telephone on a highly reflective desktop.

His ribbed socks, aubergine in color, were partially concealed by the knife-sharp crease of rich grey trouser legs, a grey more colorful than screaming electric blue.

Vanessa Savage had indeed seen it all, though Khartovski and myself assuredly had not. She travelled as one to whom travelling vast distances had long become incessant and its ever-recombinative nuances a matter of indifferent habit. For her, every difference was ever the same, every picture told the same jetlagged, unchanging story: exponentially increased numbers of human ciphers on a rubber treadmill upon which treading was neither necessary nor desirable, a white space on a page of passing time, and as we had virtually no luggage, no encumbrances to drag with us or deal with retrieving, our passage through immigration and customs involved merely standing on line, surrendering documents to indifferent uniformed bipeds, a stroll to what signage still indicated as "Ground Transportation."

She told the taxi driver: "The New International Zone, Quadrant Five, three thousand eleven Sample Street."

The female driver, more to herself than Vanessa, half-whispered, "Mother Gin-Sling's Casino, Open 24 Hours." The automatic pistol in the driver's door recess Vanessa eyed as an expected amenity, the kind of weapon she'd seen in a thousand taxis without raising an eyelid higher in surprise.

"Everything we say is being monitored," she apprised us, "but not to worry. Everything anyone says anywhere is being monitored, recorded, stored for reference. This is, after all, our brave new world."

"Brave?" I queried. I had even shed my stammer.

"Sam, it's a figure of speech. And true. One has to be brave to live in all of this, it's not a world for sissies."

"No sissies in this taxi," Khartovski laughed, his Russian accent having thickened during the flight in increments.

"Life and death isn't a business for sissies," Vanessa said. "I use the singular because they're the same thing."

"I'm no sissy," the driver interloped.

"Shut up and drive," Vanessa snapped. "You aren't part of this conversation, either."

The driver shuddered.

"Or you wouldn't be driving a cab, now, would you?"

"That's harsh," Khartovski said.

"I'm harsh," replied Vanessa. "As the scorpion told the frog mid-river, it's my nature."

She then issued a stream of dexterously inflected Chinese to the driver, who merely nodded, negotiating the motorway with what must have been enviable skill and a faint smile.

"No regrets, I hope," Vanessa asked Khartovski and myself in turn.

"Never ask, never worry," I said.

"Never ask, stay intact," responded Vanessa.

The New Old City jumped into view.

"You wouldn't recall when they replaced Hollywood Boulevard with Hollywood Boulevard," Vanessa sighed. "But it's the same, it's the same, it's the same. Simulacrum upon simulacrum, a fossil in amber."

As we turned down Sample Street and pulled up near the casino, Vanessa's face turned unreadable, a mask of sorts, on which you could project nearly any mood or cogitation. As if she were shutting down, closing up shop in some area of her mind.

"You know," she said, "when you've seen the same movie a certain number of times, you stop paying much attention to what's going on in the narration. You see the furniture, the ornamentation of the sets, and, if you've been in it once too often, you find you can't play your part with much conviction."

"I think I understand," I said. "You don't need to get whapped with a loop needle."

"Ah, you know about looping, Sam. I knew there was more behind that speech defect than met the eye."

25

The dimensions of the casino were confusing enough without the auditory horror vacuui of pinging and clicking of roulette balls and the gurglings of slots machines, the incessant human traffic across its intricately patterned carpets, from rows of slots to cashier counters, changing shifts of croupiers, the customers a mixture of every nationality and type and the tiered arrangement of playing areas. The chandeliers pendant from the ceiling, the waitresses delivering drinks to the players, the attendants distributing cups of coinage, and the absolute obliteration of time.

Vanessa led us through the maze of it all, to what could hardly be termed a quiet corner, but into a slightly less congested labyrinth of velvet curtains, nightclub tables, bars, and salons: we marched along what I perceived to be a ramp, a second area spiralling across the first like a strand of a DNA helix, until we reached a kind of theater balcony overlooking the vast main roulette table: there, in an alcove, were Petrie, Smith, a forbidding-looking woman in a sarong draped in a glittering wrap whose hair defied gravity, and a Eurasian girl who looked unsettlingly familiar, nearly Vanessa's twin but for her duskier skin… and Marco Dominguez, whom I had thought we'd left behind at Land's End.

"Mother," Vanessa addressed the Dragon Lady, "I'd like you to meet Samuel and Misha Khartovski."

"Welcome, gentlemen, I believe you know Dr. Petrie and Inspector Smith. And my husband, Marcellus Dominguez."

"Marco? How on earth did you get to Shanghai?"

"The same way you get to Carnegie Hall, Sam. Practice, practice."

"Through another portal, I'll wager," said Weymouth Smith.

"All portals lead to Shanghai," said the woman who now introduced herself as Mother Gin-Sling. "What the others have in common," she told Smith, "is that they've all come here from an English shipping village, not unlike Shanghai in its early days. Marcellus was sent there from West Africa, to monitor what one of my emissaries had assured me was an ideal location from which to extend our operations."

Mother Gin-Sling glided about the balcony, which dilated as she did so into an immense dining room, where the décor resembled the ornate patterning of the casino's eye-dazzling arrangement of filigreed metals and jai-tech, lined with bronze lifesize figures.

"For years, Smith, you have been jousting with shadows."

Vanessa and the Eurasian girl embraced each other. Or, initially, locked together in a hug. And then… they merged, like two holograms creating a single image.

"When we left Land's End – " Khartovski, or Misha, whose first name I had never known, began to say.

"There is no Land's End, Mr. Khartovski, as we now realize. The village, the brothels, the fallow shipbuilding waterfront, the harbor, the ships: why and how you slipped into the illusion of it I cannot say, but the Council of Those That Know thought it best in their wisdom to appoint one of my rivals, now my employee, to conjure it from bits and pieces of what remained of the Industrial Revolution."

"Did you mean to say," asked Smith, "that even Fu Manchu does not exist?"

"Of course he exists," Mother Gin-Sling replied. "He has always existed, a weaver of intrigues, hallucinations, false memory loops, and much else besides."

Now a uniformed waiter entered the expanding space, carrying a tray of liqueur glasses.

"Inspector Smith, have you ever considered that Dr. Fu Manchu, however many dire circumstances he has placed you in, has always spared your life?"

"I'd just been wondering that aloud to Petrie here, only an hour ago."

"An hour ago? Are you certain that an hour has passed since you walked 'unwittingly' into Fu Manchu's trap?"

"Certainly before Vanessa and Ken Jay brought us to the portal. Before we left the dungeon in Paraguay."

"Mother," said the former Vanessa, now a composite being, "I think we now have a sculptoric group."

"We have the configuration of one," said Marco, Marcellus, whatever his name was.

"In no-space, in timelessness, everything that occurs has already occurred. And, will occur again. Somewhat differently, yet forever the same. My daughter Viola will explain it to you."

And then Mother Gin-Sling and Marcellus retracted, there is no other word for it: the space of the casino where they stood disappeared.

We now stood quite close to the spiral balcony, while below, a number of players laid chips on quadrants of the roulette table.

"Drink up," Viola said. We four men, holding liqueur glasses, obediently quaffed an ambrosial mixture of unfamiliar tincture: Of opium? Of some arcane essence?

My attention fixed itself on the spinning roulette wheel and the little white ball whirling inside it. I experienced the sensation that I was the whizzing roulette ball, that the numbers I passed in my spin were the faces of all those I had known at Land's End, and before: that I was myself and Petrie, that Smith and Fu Manchu were the same imago, and that the spin would never stop, the ball that was me would never come to rest on red or white, on 7 or 24, but rotate for eternity on that clicketing wheel.

"Sam," I heard Viola call from an immense distance, "we think we inhabit two different modes of being, that of consciousness and the dream state. But we must learn to think of these as a unitary field – what Husserl calls *a field of sensuous data*."

I'm either dreaming all this or I'm losing my mind, I thought.

"You are dreaming all this," Viola's voice whispered, "but you are finally finding your mind, in the most practical way. Forgive me, my darling, for again citing Husserl, but this does apply to what has happened. *All immediate association is an association in accordance with similarity. Such association is essentially possible only by virtue of similarities, differing in degree in each case, is up to the limit of complete likeness. Thus all original contrast also rests on association: the unlike comes to prominence on the basis of the common. Homogeneity and hetereogeneity, therefore, are the result of two different and fundamental modes of associative unification. Another mode of unification, different from either of these, is the unification of the present and the not present. It is only by associative blending that a field of sense is a unity; likewise, its order and articulation, as well as all formation of groups and likenesses, are produced in the field by the effect of association: the similar is evoked by the similar, and it contrasts with the not similar.*"

The casino once more imposed its architectural intricacies on my awareness. For down in the roulette pit, despite the vast distance separating the balcony I stood on from the croupier, I could see the gamblers as clearly as if observing them through a telescope: the croupier bore an uncanny resemblance to the auto dynast Colly Colecrupper; the dwarf Thalidomido, or someone very like him, in a smartly tailored suit and patterned Sulka tie, was placing chips on 5, 29, and a side bet on rouge; the fartsome abortionist, Philidor Wellbutrin, seemed doubled in another well-tailored figure wearing a monocle, observing the play, and after the wheel was given its initial spin, quickly placed a neat stack of 100 dollar chips on 41; at tables in the tiers above the gaming table, observing the action, ordering champagne from the waiters, sipping from crystal flutes, I noted others who could well have been duplicates of persons from Land's End: Erna Cuntze, for example, enjoyed the attentions of a fair and comely youth in a tuxedo jacket and Levi denims, while still others bearing a close correspondence to inhabitants of the squalid village I had adopted as my own – for I, Sam, had now merged with Dr. Petrie, indeed *was* both Petrie and Sam (I preferred Sam to Obregon, if truth be told) – had the inescapable sensation that, standing there with my arm around the ravishing Viola's boyishly lanky waist, had always been in this casino, had never left this casino, and that Khartovski, no longer coughing his lungs up but looking elegant and well-exercised as he stood nearby, and Weymouth Smith, whose visage had passed through bewilderment to amusement, through amusement to perplexity, perplexity to understanding, greeted me from a balcony opposite our helixlike strand of the casino architecture, querying none other than the slain, large-nosed Fanny Bacon, the slain prostitute, with an almost fey little wave.

"Strange to tell, Viola, I understand exactly what you just cited from that philosopher."

"Paraphrased, really."

"But tell me, if you can: have I dreamed my life entirely, or has any of it been real?"

Viola stepped away from my embrace and ran her fingertips along the narrow edge of the balcony.

"Why do you separate your dreams from your life? Divide reality from your waking and sleeping perceptions? I've just explained, or tried to, at least, that they run along exactly the same continuum. Both are real, and are the same, but your mind has trained itself, somehow, to perceive them as different orders of reality. They belong to the same stratum of illusion."

"And they begin and end in the same place?"

"To be more correct, Sam, they begin and end in no place, and transpire in no time. Somewhere, meaning no where, Weymouth Smith and yourself are thwarting the schemes of Dr. Fu Manchu, who is both death and life, and who carries out the will of my mother, Mother Gin-Sling, who is both Eros and Thanatos, a kind of secular living goddess. But look here, why take all this so solemnly, when we could simply move to the other strand of the helix and play a few games of blackjack?"

207

"Why not poker?" Mother Gin-Sling appeared suddenly between us. "You lost a good deal the last time you visited my emporium, Sam Petrie."

"I didn't come tonight to win it back, I assure you," I heard myself saying, though my voice sounded unfamiliar to my inner ear.

At a card table, as champagne was being poured by an adorable Chinese youth all round, Khartovski dealt cards to each of us: Viola, Mother Gin-Sling, Smith, the redoubtable Ken Jay, and Fanny Bacon, whom I now recognized as Dixie Pommeroy: the so-called chorus girl whose deception had cost me my medical license. Dixie had a sharp Brooklyn accent and a way with a beret and a cigarette holder.

"Anything... wild?" she asked the general assembled company.

"Only the joker," said Mother Gin-Sling.